How It Was in Hawk Creek Canyon

by
Mollie Elizabeth Nicholson

DORRANCE PUBLISHING CO., INC.
PITTSBURGH, PENNSYLVANIA 15222

ISBN # 0-8059-5912-2

Printed in the United States of America

First Printing
For information or to order additional books, please write:
Dorrance Publishing Co., Inc.
643 Smithfield Street
Pittsburgh, Pennsylvania 15222
U.S.A.
1-800-788-7654
Or visit our web site and on-line catalog at *www.dorrancepublishing.com*

To my late husband, Earl, who was my husband for sixty-seven
years, my best friend forever,
and who understood me better than anyone else.

ෂ❀ও

Contents

ഇൗൽ

Acknowledgments

80C3

*M*any have contributed in so many ways to make the publication of this book possible. For their talents, inspiration, perseverance and patience, some must be mentioned by name:

- My many, many friends and family who have been supportive in their prayers and encouragement along the way.
- My granddaughters, Toni Bukowski and Carrie Manley, for their time helping with the editing.
- My two sons, Merle (Nick) Nicholson and Bruce Nicholson.
- Laurie Larsen of Renton Secretarial Service for the many hours of typing, set-up and computer support.
- Karen Harlow for making the mailing labels.
- Bob Sexauer for his artwork.
- And, most of all, my husband, Earl, who was together with me while I wrote this book.

Mollie Nicholson

Introduction

ഓരു

*H*ow It Was at Hawk Creek Canyon is an intimate story of family life in Eastern Washington on a canyon farm in Lincoln County during the 1920s.

The author, Mollie Nicholson, was awarded the Lucille McDonald Memorial Award by the Pacific Northwest Writers' Conference in July 1993, on the merits of several chapters of this book submitted in that special category.

With a Welsh mother and a North Carolinian father, Nicholson describes her childhood home as a crosswalk of inherited backgrounds from the heather hills of Wales and the tobacco plantations of the South.

Childhood on the Hawk Creek farm was tinted with hues of Welsh traditions and superstitions and seasoned with the spicy flavor of deep South philosophy, a mixed heritage as different as chalk and cheese.

Chapter One
A Welsh Grandmother
ℰℭ℞

*E*ven at the age of eleven, I was fully aware of my mixed heritage from grandparents as different as chalk and cheese. My home was a crosswalk of inherited backgrounds from the heather hills of Wales and the tobacco plantations of the southern states.

With Mama a Welshman and Papa a North Carolina Tarheel, my childhood was tinted with the hues of British tradition, seasoned with the spicy flavor of deep South philosophy, and often disturbed with bits of old country superstitions. These family characteristics became very evident when I made my first trip to the cemetery with my Welsh grandmother.

The day before Memorial Day, May 29, 1922, Grandma and I had come to Davenport early in the morning to decorate the graves for the next day's services. Slowly and silently we made our way between the tombstones until we reached the family plot.

The cemetery was located some distance from Davenport, surrounded by fields which, in a period of almost forty years, Grandma had seen change from native prairie grasses to cultivated farm land. Since 1887 this part of eastern Washington had been home to her and her family.

As we stood beside the family plot, she reached out and took my hand. Tears in Grandma's eyes kept me from asking questions. She alone held treasured memories of those who lay beneath the prairie sod.

Grandma was past seventy, hale and hearty, and loyal to her Welsh heritage. Trips to her home were highlights of my girlhood. It was her idea to take me to the cemetery so I could learn the meaning and significance of Memorial Day.

My family lived in Hawk Creek Canyon, seven miles from Grandma's house. This distance did not prevent her from coming for me with horse and buggy. It took her persuading and my begging to get Papa and Mama to agree to let me go to the cemetery.

Mama said, "You better ask your Papa, but if you go I want you to act like a little lady and be of some 'elp."

As the oldest of five children, even though only eleven years old, I was needed at home to help Mama take care of the little ones. Papa reluctantly granted me permission to go, saying, "Why in tarnation couldn't she go there alone? No need to drag you along. Yer needed here. Blame it all, anyway! Well, jist git goin' and when you git there, try to be of some he'p." And so it was, the next morning, my Welsh grandmother and I went to the Davenport cemetery.

As we stood beside the family graves, Grandma wiped the tears from her eyes and continued to hold my hand. We stood together looking down at a little marker. The stone was flat and smooth and cold.

"This is the grave of your little brother," reflected Grandma as she clasped my hand more firmly. "And, but for the mercy of God, your mother would be 'aving a marker, too."

"My little brother?"

"Yes, Mollie. You know, you aren't the oldest one in the family. There was a little boy born the year before you came along. Your mother was never to 'ave any more children. Three doctors said so. I 'eard them tell your father. I can remember as if it were only last night. A fine baby boy...a Welshman if I ever saw one...never got 'is chance to breathe a breath of life...and your mother lying there like an angel 'erself."

"Oh, Grandma! You don't mean there's a baby under the dirt!"

"No, child. Only a little coffin. The baby has gone 'ome to Jesus...and your mother almost went with 'im. She was never supposed to 'ave you, or any of the rest of you that keep coming along every year or so. Your father wanted a big family and it looks like that stubborn Southerner is going to 'ave it 'is way."

I did not know about the little baby who had gone home to Jesus but I did know I loved Papa and Mama, and I loved my grandparents very much. While we were looking down at the little stone marker, I closed my eyes very tightly and silently prayed, Jesus, forgive me for being born when they didn't want me and I wasn't supposed to be.

Laying her hand on the big family tombstone, Grandma continued, "This is your grandpa's grave. 'E died when your mother was just a young girl. Your grandpa and I were youngsters together in Wales. When 'e came to America I promised to follow and become his bride, and that I did, in a little mining town in Pennsylvania. My 'eart goes back many a time, but I 'aven't set foot on Welsh soil since the day I set sail for America."

I could tell Grandma's thoughts were far away across the ocean in a little town called Tailbach, which means "little houses" in Welsh. Now I knew why there was such a wistful note in her beautiful voice when she would sing for us, "I'll Take You Home Again, Kathleen" or "God Be with You Till We Meet Again."

As we busied ourselves with the task of cleaning up the accumulation of weeds, Grandma continued to reminisce. "Yes, I saw this country change from a territory to a state, and from bunchgrass prairie 'omesteads to prosperous wheat farms. I pulled many a pile of wool grass when the prairie sod was broken.

"There was a mortgage," Grandma informed me. "I paid it off and finished the payments on the h'eighty h'acres. I kept the 'orses and sold off some of the cattle and the wheat. Even took your mother with me and worked on a cook wagon fixing meals for a threshing crew. That fall I kept a boarder for fifteen cents a meal. 'E was building the school'ouse. That was the fall I bought this tombstone.

"We must never fail to pay our respects to the dead. There's a h'empty spot there beside your grandpa. They'll be layin' me there one of these days. Yes, child. The young may go but the old must go."

Grandma's Welsh roots were firmly transplanted. This land belonged to her and she belonged to the land. Throughout the morning hours we pulled stray weeds and raked level the gravel inside the cement curbing, stopping only long enough to pass the time of day with old timers who had come to prepare their family plots.

As Grandma talked with her neighbors and friends, I could not help but think of my other grandparents whose roots were not so secure in the soils of Washington. They had a family plot, too, far away in North Carolina. Papa realized how they felt and would remark, "It isn't easy for Ma and Pa out here. They jist can't he'p thinkin' of what they left down South. Why, Pa was past seventy-five when they left North Carolinar to come out here to Warshington."

Whenever Grandma and Grandpa talked of their home in the South, there was a lonesome look in their eyes and a homesick note in their voices. They had come west because a devoted family of children did not want to leave them behind.

Papa told me that when his folks arrived in Davenport from North Carolina, he met them at the station to take them to his home on Hawk Creek. His ma was tired and miserable and the country, to her, looked strange and unwelcoming. As they started down Hawk Creek Canyon, jolting along over rough dirt roads, it seemed more than she could bear. Grandpa was too exhausted to comment but Grandma, it seemed, was never too tired to complain. As they started down a steep, winding hill with the yawning canyon ahead, she turned to Papa and said, "Where in tarnation are ye takin' us? Lawsee me! This must be the world's hind end."

Thoughts of Papa's folks were soon put aside for there was work to be done in the graveyard. I was sent to borrow a bucket to carry some water for the flowers we had brought to put in fruit jars. We had forgotten to bring a pail but we could not go back to get it once we had started out on the road. Grandma said it would bring bad luck to go back after we had set out on a journey. I had learned to abide by Grandma's superstitions, more out of love for Grandma than in fear of all the bad luck that would be heaped upon us.

When we had finished our work in the cemetery, it was nearly noon and the May sun was getting quite warm. We gave Old Billy some hay from the back of the buggy, spread a quilt on the grass, and sat down to eat our lunch. There were hard-boiled eggs and butter sandwiches. Any sandwich was good when it was made with Grandma's homemade bread. I could never forget the way she prepared them-with the loaf securely anchored under her arm, she would spread the end of the bread with butter and then proceed to cut off a slice, repeat the procedure, and make a sandwich. Bara ymenyn, she called it.

When I reached for the salt to use on my hard-boiled egg, I knocked over the salt shaker. I did not wait for Grandma to tell me; I threw some salt over my left shoulder. There was no use taking a chance of having a quarrel with someone. Then I carefully and obviously crushed the egg shells under the heel of my shoe, although it required a teaspoon to do it properly. I felt if this practice could bring the fishing boats of Wales safely into port, perhaps it would furnish for Grandma and me a safe return home. Besides, I wanted to make it obvious to Grandma the Welsh "half" was showing.

As we returned home that afternoon, we did not stop in town. We drove Old Billy along the road that followed the creek. Grandma entertained me with a running commentary concerning the countryside.

"This is the beginning of the creek that runs through your place, way northwest of 'ere. This is Cottonwood Creek. Davenport used to be called Cottonwood Springs. The creek must have been named for the trees. Another stream comes in from the south, at the Rookstool place. Don't know why they call it 'Awk Creek from there on down, unless they had more 'awks than they had cottonwoods."

The afternoon sun grew hotter and Old Billy went more slowly. The buggy wheels cut into the dusty road and the horse's hooves sounded muffled in the soft dirt. We waved to some men working in a small patch of land between the creek bed and the road. Just beyond them was a wooden bridge. The horse and buggy made a big rumbling noise as we rolled over the wooden planks. It made me think of the Billy Goats Gruff and I wondered if there could be a troll under the bridge. For one moment I was sure that there was.

With a loud whoop, three naked boys dashed from beneath the bridge. They ran up the bank, their wet bodies glistening in the sunshine. They may have been inhabitants of the old swimmin' hole, but Old Billy considered them first-rate trolls. He took the bit in his mouth and we were off-not down the road, but up the side of the hill as far as the roadway would permit. Finally he stood quivering with the buggy behind him tipped to a precarious angle.

I was dreadfully frightened and had similar nightmares for nights to come. Through it all, Grandma never lost command of the situation but she did lose command of her dignity. She was not so concerned about the runaway horse as she was about the indecent exposure of the young males from under the bridge.

"If I could catch those young gentlemen, I'd take this buggy whip to their backsides. There is a young lady present in this buggy."

"Just leave them to me," urged the farmer, who had come running from the field beyond the bridge and was leading the prancing Old Billy back down the hillside to the roadway. Grandma and I remained on the buggy seat throughout the rescue operations. Her face was red as she added indignantly, "This is my granddaughter, and we are raising 'er up to be a little lady. She's not used to such goings on." I knew then she was not aware my brothers swam in the nude whether I was present or not, and occasionally, when Mama had not known about it, my sister and I had tried it ourselves. It was easier to swim without clothes than with old dresses pinned between our legs with safety pins.

The farmer had a twinkle in his eye as he accepted Grandma's thanks and saw us safely on our way. Old Billy was a bit more skittish the rest of the way home. A jackrabbit dashing across the road gave us a sudden jolt but, after a few words of Welsh-which Old Billy seemed to understand better than I did-we were wheeling along up the hill, away from the creek road and out across the prairie.

We could see the windmill in the distance. The blades of the wheel were motionless, which meant that the water trough could be empty and there might be some pumping to be done. Travel seemed to go slowly across a level stretch until Grandma started singing, in her wonderful voice, a song she and Grandpa used to sing together in the past years. It went something like this:

> "This world is a difficult riddle,
> For 'ow many people you see
> Whose faces are long as a fiddle
> Who ought to be singing with glee.
> What is the use of repining?
> For where there's a will there's a way,
> Tomorrow the sun may be shining
> Although it looks cloudy today."

It made me happy to hear Grandma singing. I realized what a grand person she was, putting away the sadness of the day and making ready to face the future with a song, ready to take whatever fate should bring and willing to meet it head on and with a smile. Just as Papa had often said, "Where there's a will, there's a Welshman."

It was mid-afternoon; Old Billy was in the barn, and I was sharing a cup of tea with

Grandma. At home I had to drink milk, but at Grandma's I had tea four times a day if I wanted it. I added lots of cream and sugar and always asked for a refill.

No one could make tea to suit Grandma. The teapot had to be scalded and fresh water brought just to the boiling point, then poured quickly over two pinches of Grandma's special mixture of English teas. She made her own blend of "gunpowder" and "spider leg." When I held some in my hand it looked like little green bullets and black spiders' legs. After the hot water was poured over the tea, a little knitted skirt affair, called a "cozey" was placed over the teapot to keep the contents hot.

After our lunch of tea and cheese sandwiches, Grandma rested in her big high-backed rocker. She liked to have her hair brushed and combed. I removed the pins and let her hair fall about her shoulders. Her hair was soft and there were never any tangles, so I invented some by bringing the comb down and picking up a few ends, bringing them up, and then down again to make little knots, so as to make Grandma believe there was much more combing and brushing to be done.

Grandma grew tired of the tangles and told me to clean out the brush and comb while she pinned up her hair. I started to go outside to throw the combings away but was quickly stopped.

"Don't throw it out there! Put it in the 'air receiver on my dresser. If you throw that 'air outdoors the birds will be making nests of it and I'll be 'aving an 'eadache. I save the combings and then send them away to be made into rats. Ladies buy them to put in their pompadours."

As I put the hair into the receiver on the dresser, I noticed that by the little alarm clock it was only four o'clock, and I was feeling as if it were bedtime.

"Grandma, this has been a long day since we got up this morning."

"Well, h'it's the last of May and the days are getting longer. Cam ceiliog, we say in Wales. It means the sunlight is a little longer each day by just the length of time it takes a rooster to step. Cam ceiliog means step of a rooster. The days may seem long to you but they go too fast when a person's my h'age."

Grandma rocked for awhile, then dozed off to sleep. I started for the porch, but stopped under the horseshoe that hung above the door. It was a real horseshoe, wrapped in green silk and hanging with the points up to keep the good luck in.

Papa said Grandma's horseshoes were a lot of stuff and nonsense. He said horseshoes were made for horses to wear and not for parlor decorations for superstitious old ladies.

I tiptoed out the door. Grandma needed to rest. It had been an exciting day and tomorrow would be the Memorial Day services.

Chapter Two
Decoration Day

ഉറ

While Grandma dozed in her chair, I sat on the front steps of the porch. The day at the cemetery had been emotionally trying for me. It had changed the concept of my ancestors from ancient history to reality. In my short lifetime, death had not entered my realm of experience. Death was something people talked about or something which occurred on the farm as a natural or man-inflicted happening among the animals.

I felt tired and sleepy but it did not seem safe to take a nap with Grandma dozing in her rocker. After all, this was a lonesome place with just Grandma and me, for at home there was always "the whole kit and snaggle of us," as Papa's folks would say.

The sun had started to go down behind the house where it kicked up quite a splash of color before retiring for the night. As I sat there in the shadows waiting for Grandma to awaken, I tried to remember how long it took a rooster to step. It would soon be the month of June and the longest day of the year, and that old rooster would soon have to start backing up. A rooster step! Even with little marks in the dirt, I could not think of this as a measure of time, so I decided to track down old chanticleer when we fed the chickens later on.

Stretching out from the house was the prairie, as Grandma called it, although it was more of a rolling plain than a prairie. Formerly covered with bunchgrass and sagebrush, it was now a checkerboard of wheat fields and summer fallow. I looked out across the endless acres of young green wheat and bordering fields of gray-brown land recuperating from last year's crop.

I looked up and down the roads and, as far as I could see, no one was in sight. Three roads met at Grandma's gate, two from Davenport and one from Hawk Creek. The Hawk Creek road went on down the canyon for about twelve miles to the little town of Peach, where the creek flowed into the Columbia River.

It was along this Hawk Creek road that Papa and Mama met for the very first time. I had often heard Mama say it was at the lower pasture gate she had seen Papa coming along the road. Then Papa would tease Mama by saying, "Yep, your mama was out there hangin' on the gate post awaitin' for some man to come along, so when she saw me it jist swept her off'n her feet."

Mama would interrupt and say, "Now you know it wasn't like that. I didn't even know your name or who you were and it was a long time before I ever saw you again."

As soon as I heard Grandma stirring in the house, I went right in to see if she could remember when Mama and Papa had met.

"Why sure, gel, I can remember when they met. Why would you be askin' me that?"

"Well, was Mama just hanging on a gatepost waiting for some man to come along?"

"Nonsense! Whatever put such a notion into your 'ead?" questioned Grandma as she tied a big apron over her dress and started picking up the remains of our lunch. Going on with her work, she continued to do some explaining to get Mama off the gatepost and to show her disapproval of Papa's sense of humor.

Grandma told me that one summer evening back in 1905 when Mama was bringing the cows from the lower pasture, a strange man stopped by the gate and asked which road he should take to Davenport. Now, all this seemed so romantic to me because I had gathered from family comments that Mama had been a pretty young Welsh girl and Papa a very eligible bachelor or, according to Papa's self-appraisal, "a Scotch-Irish Tarheel, footloose and fancy free."

"Yes, your mother and father met out there by the road. When your Mother came back to the 'ouse from getting the cows that evening, she told me that she had directed a strange man as to the road 'e should be taking to town. But the mystery of it all, 'e was driving a team which was belonging to a neighbor man."

"Now, Grandma, don't tell me that Papa was a horse thief."

"It isn't polite to be interrupting! Your Father was looking to buying a farm and had borrowed the team for a trip to town." Then Grandma went on to tell me that Papa's visit to that part of the state of Washington was, at that time, a brief one. After that he had spent some time traveling and working in Oregon and California before he returned to Davenport to buy the canyon farm and claim the Hawk Creek "schoolmarm" as his bride.

While Papa had been traveling and looking for a likely nesting place, Mama had been changing from a prairie flower to a full-blown school teacher. Grandma cared very little about the details of the family romance but she was concerned with the grandchildren, whom she had helped usher into the world, nursed through illnesses, and come to love with all her big generous heart.

As evening wore on and the chores were completed, Grandma turned to me with all her fervor for cleanliness. "Take off all your clothes and 'op into the tub of water," she said, filling a wash tub from the reservoir on the back of the cookstove. This was the usual routine when I visited Grandma for an overnight stay.

"While you're bathing I'll wash out your underclothes," she continued, handing me a fragrant bar of soap and a big snowy bath towel. That meant I would have to wear an old wrapper of hers until bedtime or at least until my hair was dry. An egg shampoo always followed the tubbing.

Grandma's tub was much larger than ours at home. It was a delight to slosh around in the water without getting my knees hooked under my chin. Grandma supervised my bathing. She scrubbed my back, which she felt was a sadly neglected part of the bath routine.

"Cleanliness is next to Godliness," she reminded me, emphasizing each word with a swish of the washcloth until I fairly squeaked as I stepped from the tub, keeping my distance from the hot cookstove.

I remembered only too well the evening Papa had come too close to the stove. He had just finished his bath and was bending over to dry his toes, when his shrieks of pain rallied the whole family to attention. Mama promptly said, "Now never mind, children, run on back to bed. Your Papa just go too close to the stove." It was only a little while later that we heard her laughing and saying, "Better look where you are stooping next time. You've got the words 'Home Comfort' branded backwards right across your bottom."

As I watched Grandma dump the slightly soiled bath water out the back door, I felt I was enjoying real extravagance. At home, bath time was sort of a relay race. We started with the smallest and worked up to the oldest or dirtiest one of the children. Since I was the oldest, bath time at Grandma's was a real treat.

By bedtime my hair was dried and plaited into two tight coronet braids. My shoes were shined and my clothes were clean and ready for morning. Grandma had a new hat trimmed with lavender flowers to wear with her best black dress. Tomorrow would be Decoration Day, a time for bands, bouquets, and military ceremonies.

We got up very early the next morning and were among the first to arrive at the cemetery for the Memorial Day services. It was important, solemn, and a little bit frightening. The bugles reminded me of the poem I had learned at school. This was the first time I had ever heard a bugle and only then, for me, did the words of that poem begin to have a real meaning, "Blow, bugle, blow; set the wild echoes flying."

There were new flags on the soldiers' graves. This was of great concern to me. The soldier I knew best of all was my grandpa, Papa's father, a veteran of four years in the Confederate army. When I asked if he would have a flag on his grave if he should die, I was told he had fought against his country, that he was a rebel, and that flags were only for American soldiers.

The rest of the ceremonies did not impress me very much. I was concerned about my grandpa. He would deserve a flag if any man ever would. Someday I planned to write to the president of the United States and plead Grandpa's case.

Some soldiers fired guns over the graves. It seemed dreadful to make so much noise in the cemetery where all should have been peace and quiet. I jumped every time they fired, even though they were shooting over our heads. It reminded me of the way Grandpa had fought in the Civil War. He furnished a military salute for each battle he was in as he fired over the heads of the Union soldiers.

"You know," he told me, "I never knowingly shot a man. The Bible teaches 'Thou shalt not kill', and for four long years I kept that commandment."

Then, chuckling to himself and stroking his white beard, he would add, "Guess I must have been the poorest shot in the hull Confederacy."

Grandpa had really contributed to Union victory. By firing over the heads of the Yankees, he had wasted a lot of his country's enemy ammunition, and he had certainly not added to the Union casualty list. Therefore, I reasoned, Grandpa would deserve a flag.

There was the memory of one incident that remained to trouble Grandpa's conscience. He could never forget it. "Once I was detailed to a farin' squad at a court martial. I'll never know if my rifle held the fatal bullet that killed that there deserter.

"Our guns were taken from us as soon as the guilty man had fallen. I prayed for that slain boy and I asked God's mercy on my soul, knowin' full well that had I refused to carry out orders I'd a been dealed the same fate."

When the Memorial Day services were over, people stood in little groups and talked. Grandma introduced me to some of her friends.

"This is my granddaughter, Mary's oldest child. She's tall for her h'age, don't you think?" Then there followed a discussion as to which side of the family I took after. They never could agree and I was not sure if I looked like a Yankee or a Confederate.

The evening of the Memorial Day was a welcome time. Grandma and I were weary. We did not talk much as we did the chores but we did make plans for her to take me home. Tomorrow we would go down Hawk Creek Canyon. It was always good to visit Grandma, but after two days away from Mama and Papa I was getting a little homesick.

Chapter Three
Memories of Wales

𝔰𝔬𝔠𝔯

*T*he next morning before Grandma and I were ready to go down the canyon, Papa came by on his way to town. I ran out to meet him as soon as I heard the rumble of the wagon and recognized Flaxie and Lizzie, our best team of mares.

"Well, how's my girl?" asked Papa, tying the team to the fence and looking down at me with those sky-blue eyes. "The eyes are the windows of the soul," Mama often said, and through Papa's blue windows I could see a soul of many moods, usually happy and jovial, but violently perturbed when angered and deep in despair when saddened. Today his eyes reflected the blue of the heavens and showed only tenderness and love for his little girl who was standing by the very road where he had first seen Mama many years before.

Papa patted me on the shoulder and said, "I'm going into Davenport this mornin' to fetch out a load of supplies. I reckon you kin stay here with yer Grandma. Watch out for that horse! Yer goin' to git trampled on!" he warned as I was giving Flaxie and Lizzie a few affectionate pats. I was lonesome, even for the horses.

I could see Papa was ready for a busy day, dressed in a pair of new bib overalls over a blue chambray shirt. He never wore his dark suit to town unless it was for jury duty or important business trips. His dark wavy hair showed beneath his hat, hair much darker than his reddish brown mustache. I noticed he had trimmed his mustache himself, a job usually reserved for me to do along with clipping the hair on his neck and trimming his sideburns and, occasionally, the long hairs that grew on his ears.

As we walked up the path toward the house, Grandma came out on the porch, drying her hands on her checkered apron and insisting, before Papa could get a word in edgewise, that he come on in and have a bit to eat.

Grandma invariably fed every person who set foot inside her gate. It was always a command performance with no refusals considered. I could never decide if it was generosity or a superstition that prompted her actions but it was public knowledge that every relative, neighbor, and passerby had a standing invitation to share her good cooking. Coaxing was not necessary. Smoke rising from Grandma's kitchen chimney made strong men drool and children complain of hunger.

"Well, it ain't been too long since I et breakfast but guess I could take time to set a spell. If it won't put you out none, I'd like to leave Mollie here today and then I'll fetch her home with me when I git back this afternoon."

"Oh, I'd keep her all summer if you'd let her stay. Sit down here by the table and I'll

11

fix you a bite to eat. How's Mary and the children?" asked Grandma as she put a cup and saucer in front of Papa and pushed the spoonholder closer to him.

"Everybody's fine. We's up most the night with the baby John. Guess he's cutting teeth. Now don't go to no extra trouble. Mmm! That coffee smells mighty good for a tea drinker to be makin'." Papa could see Grandma did not appreciate that last remark, so he went on to say, "You know some men jist eat to live but with a cook like you in the family, I jist live to eat."

Papa took time to eat a second breakfast before going on into Davenport. I stood on the porch and watched until he was out of sight. I wanted so much to go along with him but I knew better than to start coaxing, for I knew full well when Papa said something once, he meant it, and any fussing on my part would only gain for me a session of stern reproval.

Papa usually went alone on the shopping trips. Mama seldom went to town, did any shopping, or handled any of the family income. Papa had been a storekeeper prior to taking up farming and was accustomed to purchasing groceries, dry goods, and hardware. He bought all items in large quantities and the neighbors really meant it when they passed him on the road and remarked, "Well, Charlie, did you buy out the town?"

The day seemed long while I waited for Papa's return. I helped Grandma wash clothes. She had noticed the sky was red when we got up that morning and her prophecy, "Red clouds at night, sailors delight; red clouds in the morning, sailors take warning," meant a storm was brewing and we had better wash clothes while the weather was fair. We hung the lines full of billowing garments, soon blown dry by the constant wind.

The wind pulled our skirts about us as we took down the dry washing, carrying the line and clothes beyond my reach. It swept the dust of the road into little whirlwinds that danced out across the pasture. It tugged at the windmill and sent shed doors hanging shut. "Shawn Mynydd," commented Grandma, meaning the wind was only old "John of the mountains" giving vent to his wrath.

The clothes were sprinkled down and stacked in the big wicker basket. Tomorrow would be ironing day, with a hot stove heating the flat irons that would sizzle to the touch of a wet finger.

All the while we worked, Grandma was singing. She seemed to hum and sing constantly. She told me people in Wales always sang. "I can still 'ear the men going to the mines with a song on their lips. Everyone would join in and it seemed the whole village would be singing. The very 'ills seemed to catch up the melodies and drink in the feelings of the Welsh people.

"Someday, gel, you may go to Wales. If I were a few years younger I'd take ye back myself. The climate there is good for the voice. They say that Madame Patti, the h'opera singer, bought a castle at Craig-y-Nos, not far from my 'ome. She can sing better where the sea breezes bathe the 'ills. She gives concerts for the peasants as well as for the wealthy."

"Can you sing opera, Grandma?" I asked, feeling assured she had one of the best voices in the whole world.

"Well, I never tried. But a man on the boat coming h'over 'eard me singing and asked me to come to his h'office in New York and 'e'd get me a job on the stage."

"Oh, Grandma, have you been in New York?"

"I only stopped in New York long enough to get a ticket to Pennsylvania, where your grandpa was waiting for me."

"Didn't you go to see the man who was going to get you a job?" I asked with a note of disappointment. I felt Grandma had missed a real opportunity to be great like Madame Patti.

"Girls don't listen to strange men and besides, I was raised to believe that nice women don't go on the stage," said Grandma, trying to brush aside the whole incident.

"Grandma, just think. You could have had your name in the papers."

"Listen, gel. A good woman has 'er name in the papers h'only three times in 'er life, when she's born, when she marries, and when she dies."

"Well. How about Madame Patti?"

"Madame Patti was trained as a child by 'er parents, who were both talented singers. I was h'only a Welsh girl who loved to sing, and the h'only person I wanted to sing for was your grandpa, who was waiting to marry me."

"I think I'll go back to Wales someday, Grandma. Maybe it would help my voice. I'd like to sing the way you do," I said as I followed her into the living room.

The wind had quieted down and the afternoon was warm and still. Grandma sat in her rocker to rest awhile. Now that the washing was done and the clothes ready for tomorrow's ironing, there seemed to be nothing to do but to wait for Papa to return from town. I sat at Grandma's feet on the floor and continued to talk so she wouldn't doze off and leave me with that all alone feeling. I wanted her to help me plan my trip to Wales.

"Well, if you're set on going you'd better learn to speak some Welsh," laughed Grandma, knowing full well it would be a difficult task. When Grandma talked Welsh it always sounded to me as if she were gargling, there are so many guttural sounds in the language. Sometimes when Mama and Grandma would talk Welsh, Papa would say, "There they go, exercising their tonsils agin."

"You can always tell a Welshman," said Grandma. "Even when 'e is speaking h'English, the tone of 's voice will rise and fall. The Welsh people make good speakers, like Thomas Jefferson. 'Is ancestors came from Wales, from the 'ills of Snowdonia," she continued in praise of her native country. "But it is the h'Eisteddfod that has 'elped keep the Welsh language alive. It is a h'annual festival of poetry and music."

"Could I attend this festival if I get to go to Wales?"

"Yes, child, if you get to go to Wales. H'it is a long ways h'off and it isn't easy to get there. No use in wishing, for if 'orses were wishes all beggars would ride and I'd be in Wales by nightfall. You and I would go to the h'Eisteddfod and listen to the singing, the fiddlers, and the 'arpists, the pipers and the poets. We would see the Gorsedd ceremony and the crowning of the bard. Then the choir would start their singing. We would spend the whole week there listening and watching thousands of people perform, and when it was h'over we'd sing with the rest, Hen Wlad fy Nhadau, 'old land that our fathers before us held dear.'"

While I sat there at her feet, she sang in Welsh the song that brought back for her so many tender memories:

"Old mountain-built Cymru, the bard's Paradise,
The farm in the cwm, the wild crag in the skies,
The river that winds, have entwined tenderly
With a love spell my spirit in me.

Land, land,
Too fondly I love thee, dear land,
Till warring sea and shore be gone,
Pray God let the old tongue live on."

And as I listened I knew Wales was truly the "Old Land of My Fathers," and that someday I hoped to walk there and hear those Welsh voices echoed from the hills.

It was the sound of wagon wheels and the thoughts of Papa that jolted me from my reverie. Grandma wiped a tear from her cheek with the corner of her apron, and with a smile announced, "Your papa must be comin'. Run out and see if 'e can take time to come in for a bite to h'eat before you start down the canyon."

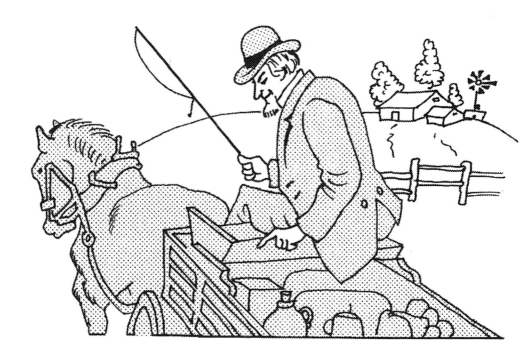

Chapter Four
Hawk Creek Canyon

෨෮෬

*P*apa did not take time for a bite to eat, although Grandma was quite insistent. It was late in the afternoon and we were a long way from the evening chores. Our home was seven miles down Hawk Creek Canyon, but not as the hawk flies. The road took the path of least resistance, which was often irregular and generally downhill.

After hurried goodbyes, we let the horses have their way for they were eager to get to the familiar stall and the feed box. Papa sat up on the high seat and I nestled down in the wagon bed among the boxes and sacks of groceries.

As we went bumping along the country road, Papa began to sing an old Southern ditty: "Tobaccy in the fore end, 'lasses in the hind, if I don't git the gal I want I'll keep my wagon agwine.

"Hop up here on the seat with me," he urged, slapping the lines down on the horses' backs for Papa, too, was anxious to get home before dark.

"I like to sit back here. Do you care if I sit on this pile of flour? Goodness sakes alive! How many sacks of flour did you get? It looks like more'n a dozen!" I exclaimed, climbing to the top of the stack.

"Git down off'n that pile of flour. You're big enough and old enough to know betterin' that. A body'd think you'd never saw a load of groceries afore. I reckon you kin set back there if you'll behave yerse'f. That's five barrels, enough to last us for quite a spell."

"Barrels? I don't see any barrels."

"Now listen here—I've told you time and agin it takes four sacks to make a barrel of flour. That's 196 pounds. A person would think you was atakin' inventory the way you're snoopin' into those groceries."

Papa guessed it right, for that was just what I was doing—taking inventory. Large cans, boxes, and sacks of things were piled on the straw that covered the bottom of the wagon bed. There was a characteristic smell about the whole load that reminded me of our big pantry at home and whetted both my appetite and my curiosity.

Beyond the pile of flour was a big roll of woven wire. When Papa noticed I was investigating the wire, he went on to explain, "That roll of waar is for a pig pen. I gotta try to keep those old long-nosed sows outa the yard. They rut up everythin' they come to. If that there waar won't hold 'em, they're gonna git rings in their noses as sure as God made little green apples. Them blamed old sows are as hard to hold in a pen as a bunch of razor backs at persimmon time."

I perched up on a five-gallon can of honey and put my feet on a fifty-pound sack of salt and looked carefully over the pile of food for something good to eat. My looking seemed to be in vain, for Papa's shopping was of a practical nature. There were two big hundred-pound sacks of white sugar and one of brown. The brown sugar was used with salt and pepper to cure the meat of those old long-nosed porkers, come butchering time. An axe handle was leaning between a bucket of axle grease and a five-gallon can of coal oil. Just beyond the roll of wire was a box with some soap, whole coffee berries, and a plug of chewing tobacco. Sometimes it was Masterpiece, Day's Work, or Horse Shoe brand, but this time it was Star chewing tobacco, and I was going to have my turn getting the little metal stars stuck in each section of the plug.

While I was thinking of the little stars on the tobacco, I spied something of which I knew Mama would never approve. Tea siftings...that cheap substitute for good tea, but for a coffee drinker like Papa, anything that would color the water was good enough to be called tea. When it came to coffee, Papa would brag, "When I want coffee, I want coffee. I've allus been accused of wantin' my coffee stronger than lye and hotter than Hell. Why, the way some folks make coffee, ye might as well dump a pound in the well and have coffee the year around. I can't understand how anybody could drink tea and then have the gall to say they really like it. They know better'n to offer me any that tea and wafer business. Why, I'd just as soon have hot air and rabbit tracks."

I did not mention the tea siftings to Papa for I knew it would send him off on a tangent and I would be in for the "coffee versus tea" lecture all of the family knew by heart. Failing to find anything good to eat among the grocery pile, I climbed up beside Papa on the wagon seat. We had started down a steep grade and he had to hold back on the lines and apply the brake until the back wheels were sliding.

"This is a mighty steep pitch we're goin' down. Look back yonder and see if that coal oil is sploshin' out. That spud gits knocked out of the spout sometimes and if that happens that flour is gonna git ruint."

We made it safely down the hill without any major mishap to the wagon load of supplies. The road leveled off again and the horses broke into a trot. "Guess these old mares have a hankerin' to git home. It is a good thing or it will be plum dark afore we git there," remarked Papa, and as the shadows lengthened and the canyon grew darker, I sat closer to him, especially when we passed one particular spot.

I could imagine wild animals were watching us from the roadside bushes as I remembered the oft-told story of a cougar Mama had seen many years ago. The story seemed to grow bigger and better as the years went by, and the cougar, in my imagination, would have made Ernest Thompson Seton sit up and take notice.

As we approached this special spot, known as Cougarville to our family, shivers trickled up and down my spine, and the little cave on the rock cliff across the way looked like a yawning cavern that might house a host of cougars. Few people had seen anything more ferocious than a pine squirrel in this vicinity since the incident, which years ago had set off a community cat-hunt, but nevertheless, each shadow seemed to suggest weird forms and every little noise seemed ready to manifest itself in that childlike scream of a cougar that at one time had echoed against the walls of this very canyon.

Often I had sat wide-eyed as Mama related the encounter with the cougar, a hair-raising episode with none of its savor lost in the retelling because Mama had the ability to lend to the incident the quality of an African safari. She would, invariably, start with a background sketch of time and place and keep us all in suspense-a family of avid listeners, fearfully anticipating a tragic ending.

The cougar story began as if it were going to be a tedious history of education. "I'll never forget that cougar or that bloodcurdling scream. That was the year I had just finished teaching the fall session of the Fitzpatrick School near Davenport and was on my way down the canyon where, the next day, I would start the winter term for the Hawk Creek School."

"At that time, districts often had short sessions, and teachers frequently taught more than one school during a year's time. In areas that could anticipate hard winters with deep, drifting snows, the schools were opened in the late summer and closed before the bad weather began. The canyon was more protected from high winds and did not have the problem of snowdrifts."

At this long, delayed beginning of the cougar incident, Mama would be interrupted by, "I thought you were going to tell us about the cougar."

"It was in the late fall," she would continue. "The days were getting shorter. It was just about dusk on a Sunday afternoon when my sister and I saw the cougar. We were riding double on our old saddle pony that trip. About halfway down the canyon I had planned to get off and walk and she was to return home with the horse. We had reached the clearing beyond the double-S curve when I decided I could walk the rest of the way. I was about to dismount and untie my belongings from the skirt of the saddle when the horse began to quiver and show his alarm.

"It was then we saw the cougar. He came walking out of the thicket and into the clearing near the road. At first I thought it was a calf or a colt, until I realized it was too low and long. As it came into full view it lowered its head, half closed its yellow-green eyes, and twitched its tail like a cat after a bird. It then let go that unearthly scream. It sounded like a child in mortal agony.

"I tried desperately to regain control of the horse as he reared and whirled. It's a wonder he didn't unseat both of us before I had presence of mind to give him some rein. My sister and I did not say a word until we were down around the S-curve. We each did not want to frighten the other."

At this point in her story, Papa would interrupt to comment, "You weren't thinkin' of each other. You'se jist too skeered to speak up. That cougar, if it was a cougar, and tain't likely it was, was probably trackin' down some other varmint. A skinny schoolmarm astride an old straw-fed horse jist didn't look very appetizin' to him."

Mama would ignore Papa's remarks and continue to describe the unsuccessful cougar hunt organized by the men of the neighborhood as the result of that incident. That was one of the first cougars seen in that area and it did cause quite a stir. Even though Papa discredited the whole story, to me cougars still lurked in the shadows of Cougarville.

Recognizing my apparent concern about the locality we were passing through, Papa allayed my fears by telling me to reach in his pocket and see what I could find. Sure enough, there was a surprise, something I had failed to locate in the groceries behind us. Both coat pockets were full of candy; one side held a sack of pink and white peppermints and the other side a couple pounds of horehound.

The cougar was soon forgotten when I started eating some of the candy. I preferred the horehound which reminded me of my favorite cough medicine. I often put on quite a spell of coughing just to get an extra spoonful. The white peppermints were always a favorite but the pink ones with the wintergreen were detestable. They were the same flavor as the worm medicine Mama got from the Watkins man. Every spring she would give all of us children a series of worm treatments just in case we were infested. If anyone of us was found picking his nose or gritting his teeth, the whole family got the works.

Uncomplainingly I would take the pink wafers, put them in my mouth, and make my way outside and out of sight. That treatment never reached its intended destination and, I suppose, if I was infested I continued to pick my nose and grit my teeth. Along with the rest, the following day, I had to take my cup of senna tea, a follow-up routine for the pink wafers. Papa always agreed with Mama that the purgative was the final and most important step in the spring purge.

Whenever one of the little boys refused the tea, Mama would delve into her treasury of knowledge and come up with such information as, "Senna is imported from India and Africa. It is called Cassia. Grandpa says it is even mentioned in the Bible."

Thereafter we all drank the senna tea, for it seemed a sacrilege not to do so. When one of my brothers asked Grandpa if this was the cup he took at communion, Mama had some more explaining to do and some punishment to administer for innocent impertinence.

As we went along in the growing dusk, Papa remarked, "I wasn't goin' to let you have none of that candy until we got home but I kinda wanted some myse'f. This is a tiresome long trip to town and back in one day. Travelin' is sort of a lark when you're young but when you git my age it's powerful tirin'."

The idea of traveling reminded me of my conversation with Grandma. "I been thinking about traveling, Papa. Do you think I could go to Wales some day?"

"To Wales? Oh sure, sure, sure! You need to go to Wales about as much as I need water in my shoes. Them pipe dreams won't git you no place. Countin' chickens afore they're hatched never put no eggs in my fryin' pan."

After those remarks we rode along in silence for awhile. I could never keep quiet for long so I tried another avenue of conversation. "I didn't know I had a little brother who was dead, one who would have been my big brother if he had lived."

"Now, who's been worryin' you about that?" asked Papa with a note of concern in his voice.

"Well, I saw his grave in the cemetery. Grandma said it was my little brother."

"Why in tarnation is there all this fuss about the dead, anyway! There's a whole world of livin' to be cared for. Jist fergit all about it. Here, take these lines and drive awhile. I got to rest these old arms of mine. Don't know what in Tom Walker I'm goin' to do if this rheumatism doesn't let up."

I took the lines while Papa rubbed his hands and pounded them on his knees to bring back the circulation. I could see the blue veins distended across the back of his weather-beaten hands. As I watched, I had the awful realization that Papa was growing old. I knew my grandparents were growing older but somehow I had blindly thought that my parents would always be the same for years to come.

Papa's age was easy to figure. He was forty years old when I was born. I could see the grey hair showing along the temples. There were even a few grey wisps in his shaggy eyebrows. His shoulders seemed to stoop more than usual as he continued to rub his hands. Papa was growing older and he needed me. It was then I wished my baby brother might have lived so he could have been the oldest child in the family.

As the road passed by our pasture fence we noticed a fence post leaning toward the ground. "I'm goin' to have to fix that tomorree," remarked Papa. "Guess you and the boys is goin' to have to he'p me. Your Mama kin spare you for a spell, at least until I kin find another hard man. That last no-count rascal jist drew his pay and walked off. Good riddance of bad rubbish, I'd say. He sure was a weak vessel."

"You mean that old fellow that came to the door begging for a job has quit already?"

"Yes, the old addle-pate left day before yesterday. He sure was a cracked pot if I ever saw one. Pretending to tell fortunes and shinin' up to the women folk. Didn't know nothin' about farmin'. Wasn't even sure which was the front end of a horse."

"He told my fortune, Papa. He said I'd be rich some day. And he told Mama she was wasting her fragrance on the desert air."

"Fragrance! Poppycock!" grunted Papa. "Your Mama wouldn't pay no 'tention to an old coot like him. Why he didn't have sense enough to pound sand in a rat hole if the directions was on the hammer handle. Jist as I said, he's good riddance of bad rubbish."

"It's gittin' so a body can't git a good hard man for love nor money. Some of these old reprobates jist hang around long enough to git a good belly full of grub and then clear out. You mark my word, that old fake-a-lou fortune teller is agoin' to end up in the asylum over at Medical Lake. It's a wonder he didn't harm one a'you younguns afore he left."

I knew Papa would not be without hired help for very long. He offered a job to any man who came in search of work, no questions asked and no recommendations needed. Papa felt every stranger was a friend in need, well deserving of food and lodging and a chance to earn a dollar. Some strangers turned out to be "desarvin' he'p" while others were just "old shitepokes," as Papa called them.

"Hop down and open the gate," came the usual command as we stopped at the entrance to the barn lot. I handed Papa the lines and got down from the wagon. The gate was a heavy wooden affair, well constructed of one-by-fours with some heavier boards of cross pieces. As I pulled back the sliding catch the heavy gate swung back free and easy on its hangings. I did not step up on the lowest board and ride back with a swish-gate swinging was done only when Papa was not present.

After the wagon and team entered the barn lot, I closed the gate and followed along behind the wagon. "It looks as if your mama and the boys have the chores tended to," called Papa as he surveyed the animals in the barn yard. My brothers had heard us coming and had the second gate open. The horses swung around into the orchard, wheeled the wagon under the apple trees, and finally came to a stop between the house and the woodshed.

Papa always made an elegant arrival. No matter how long he had traveled or how tired he was from the trip, he ended it with a flourish. The old team of mares seemed to sense the importance of a completed journey. They picked up their ears and trotted briskly up to the back door with the boys and me hanging on the tailgate of the wagon.

Mama and my sister, Grace, were standing on the porch, the cats were scampering out of the way, and the dogs were barking at the horses and giving us a rousing welcome.

"We have been waiting supper for you," said Mama. "Thought you'd be here long ago. There's a man here looking for work. I didn't know what to tell him."

"Well, put another place on the table. There's some fence to be fixed in the morning and I gotta have somebody to he'p me."

Later, while we were eating supper, I looked across the table at Papa's new "hard man" and I could not help but wonder if he was going to be a "desarving soul" or just another "old shitepoke."

Chapter Five
Mama's Fire Drill

ഇ)രു

"Hit the floor! It's daylight in the swamps," called Papa from the bedroom door. "Git up and fetch me a pair 'a stocks."

I knew Papa wanted a pair of socks, a pair that matched and without any holes. Mama tried to get Papa to say socks, but it was no use trying. It was the same way with boys' trousers, which Papa called kickers. Each time he said it, Mama would correct him and explain, in a rather indirect manner, "Your papa means knickers. That is short for knicker-brockers," to which Papa would indirectly reply, "It's a wonder your mama don't say unmentionables. How about you boys shinnying into those britches?"

When Papa called, "Git me a pair a stocks!" it was my job to dig deep into a big bag of socks that occupied a place on the closet floor beneath the stairway. This bulging sack looked like an overgrown pillowtick with a drawstring at the top. The socks were never rolled into mates. It was necessary for me to sort through these remnants and come up with some semblance of a pair, being careful that neither was minus a heel or toe. Those that needed mending I fixed with a big needle and some coarse thread, leaving a puckered bulge where there was once a hole.

Some people collect old coins, some collect stamps, but Papa collected old socks. These were part of his dowry for Mama as a bride. They were assorted sizes and colors-blues, pinkish-reds, tans, and greens. They were made of stringy cotton yarn, little resistant to wear and constantly in need of mending.

Papa, who was definitely color blind—although he would never admit it to anyone—made no attempt to pick out a pair of socks. The contrasting colors of red and green or blue and pink were very confusing to him. He trusted me to do the sorting, although I must admit I sometimes, with tongue-in-cheek and conscience twinging, handed Papa a couple of socks which he blindly accepted as mates.

The condition of Papa's sock supply was quite indicative of Mama's housekeeping—clean but not very tidy. Mama seemed to resent the monotony of keeping a house in order as she was carried along on the merry-go-round of washing, ironing, baking, churning, and having another baby.

"I've only had time to give this place a lick and a promise," Mama would hurriedly remark when Papa, who liked things neat and orderly, looked askance at the general conditions of things about the house.

As Papa stood at the door of the bedroom, the smoke from the hotcake griddle curled above his head, Mama, who had been up since dawn, could be heard banging the stove lids as she put some more wood into the fire. The kitchen was at the other end of the dining room but the tantalizing smell of the hotcakes penetrated the very walls to tickle the appetites of all the sleepyheads.

All of our family slept on the first floor. Since Mama was afraid of fire, she felt it an undue risk to have us children sleep upstairs. The two upper rooms stood unoccupied while four of us bunked in the little back bedroom within calling distance of Mama who, with Papa and the baby, slept just off the sitting room.

As Papa stood there in the doorway, after announcing the search for his pair of socks, he seemed to be contemplating some major idea. He scratched his head and scanned the room, which was originally a little kitchen before an addition had been built at the other end of the house. It was two steps down and just off the dining room and, although four of us children occupied it as sleeping quarters, it still bore the earmarks of a kitchen: a chimney, a built-in cupboard, and a shelf for a water pail and wash pan close to an outside door.

"You youngins might jist as well start sleepin' upstairs. This room will make tolable batchin' quarters fer my hard he'p. We can rig up some kind of a cook stove. That chimley is jist waiting for a little smoke."

Papa's most recent "hard he'p" had set up a few requirements to be met before our farm would be honored by his services. He had introduced himself with, "Just call me Old Bill or anything you're a mind to lay your tongue to, but give me a place where I can fix my own vittles. Now mind you," he said, hooking his thumbs under his suspenders and hiking his pants up a bit, "I'm not high-tone' or nothin' like that, but my stomach is sorta touchy. I like a place to myself and I like to cook what I want when I want it."

Papa liked this outspoken, direct approach, with no "beatin' about the bush," and assured Old Bill conditions would be altered to comply with his requests.

The first night at our place, Old Bill slept in the bunkhouse, which was no makeshift affair. It was a well-built, well-insulated building with built-in bunks and cubbyholes in which to hang clothes. The floor was pitted from hobnailed boots. An old spittoon occupied one corner near a tobacco-juice spattered wall. The place had an odor of dust and perspiration.

When occupied by hired men, the bunk house was off bounds for us children. During the busy seasons of the year, Papa often had more than one hired man. They were itinerants who came and went as the spirit moved them, with an occasional one remaining throughout the year. During the summer evenings the sounds of laughter, profanity, gambling, arguments, or an occasional sermon emerged from the half-open door. Whenever some fellow started berating the social order of our country, Papa would say, "That would-be politicianer is nothin' but an old I.W.W. I don't intend to give a mind to no triflin' sich. I'm givin' him his walkin' papers in the mornin'. He's jist the kind that 'ud set far to a man's barn or pizen his cattle."

The night Old Bill arrived, the bunkhouse was unoccupied. Papa told him to take his bed roll and spend the night out there. Now Papa, true to his promise, was going to provide a place for Old Bill to do his cooking, and the back bedroom seemed to the logical spot, so orders were issued for us children to vacate and reestablish our sleeping quarters upstairs.

The upstairs bedrooms were the two-storied cross of our t-shaped house. The side facing the road had two porches. People coming to see us had the choice of three front doors, entering either the front room, dining room, or kitchen. In front of the porches and extending the length of the house was a well-built wooden sidewalk which continued on to the apple house, then branched off and took a right angle turn to the outhouse. With three doors opening out to this sidewalk, Papa was right when he would say, "At our home, all doors lead to the backhouse!"

It was a backhouse to be proud of. The former owner's second wife had had it made to her specifications. It had been constructed by a master craftsman from accurate blueprints. We would brag to other children who came to visit, "Our backhouse is better'n your'n."

It was not necessary to go the length of the walk at night since an appropriate receptacle was kept beneath the bed for any partaker of watermelon who felt so inclined. Our old receptacle was an enameled affair, slightly chipped and rusty in spots, with a lid that clanged and rattled at the least touch. It was not at all like Grandma's Old Rosy, which was made of fancy shinca. Old Rosy has painted flowers and was high and gently curved, make a comfortable seat. When it was placed on a little rug by the bed, sounds were muffled to a discreet amount of privacy, a pleasnat contrast to the tiny tinkles of the enamelware we were privileged to share.

Each morning it was my duty to run down the boardwalk with the enameled container and see that it was properly emptied and freshened up for the next night shift. Many a time I would blush a deep scarlet as some hired man would call to me on my morning trek and ask, "What you got there—your lunch pail?" I would never answer but would make a hasty retreat out of sight behind the hop vines that covered the entryway to our very fine outhouse.

We moved upstairs that morning, enamelware and all, to vacate batching quarters for Old Bill, the new hired man who had evidently proved himself to be a very "desarving" soul right from the very first handshake. Papa ignored Mama's fire warnings and in a very short while, with the enthusiastic efforts of us children, we were moved out of the little bedroom, Old Bill had moved in, and a lock was secured on the inside door between his room and the dining room. This was not to keep Bill in his room but to keep us children out.

The first thing we did after setting up the old wooden bedsteads and putting the springs and mattresses in order was to have a rehearsal for a plan of escape in case of fire. After Papa and Old Bill had left to fix the pasture fence, Mama outlined the fire drill procedure.

Just outside the window of the front bedroom, which was assigned to Grace and me, was the roof of the front porch. It was out this window and across this roof that we were to go in single file. We were to swing out into the apple tree whose big limbs hung over the eaves of the porch. Down through the branches we were to make our way to the main tree trunk and so to the ground. Virl and Joe were to come across the hallway from the other bedroom and follow the same avenue of escape. In the event their way was blocked by fire, they had a large rope secured to the bed post, ready to be tossed out the window at the first smell of smoke.

Virl, who was two years younger than I, hurdled out the window, ran barefooted across the shingled roof, and leaped onto an extending apple branch with the agility of a jungle monkey. As he disappeared down through the apple leaves, Grace stood on the edge of the roof and called, "Wait for me! Wait for me!" Whenever Virl and I would be hurrying some place, be it to school or out across a field, Grace would come panting behind us, calling and sometimes sobbing, "Wait for me! Wait for me!"

Grace summoned her courage so she would not be left behind and swung out on a big branch. She hung in space for a second and then dropped to the big limb that afforded a pathway down to the main tree trunk and on to the ground.

By the time Grace had gone on down the tree, Virl had come back up the stairs and was impatiently waiting his second turn. Joe, the youngest in the fire drill, whimpered, "I'm afraid. The house is going to burn up. I'm afraid."

"You big baby. Quit your crying. Come on, Mollie, let's take him down." Virl's plan was easier said than done. We stood on the roof, each holding one of Joe's hands. He would not go on alone and we could not all go down together.

"Lift him up here, Mollie. I'll take him down piggyback. Hang on to my neck and don't you dare turn loose."

I followed Virl and Joe down through the tree and as I reached the ground I looked back up to see Grace standing at the edge of the roof for the second time, chewing her fingernails and calling, "Wait for me! Wait for me!"

There was a large orchard surrounding the house. The trees were old and tall and rugged. We were adept at climbing, chinning and "skinning the cat." Mama, cautious as usual and not relying on our past experiences, stood by the apple tree ready to catch anyone who bungled his escape. She gave a steady stream of admonitions and warnings. "Don't get too close to the edge of the roof....That limb could break, you know....Grace, quit that hollering. You'll catch up one of these days....Don't make him come down that tree alone. He's only three years old....Look out now, you'll push someone off that roof. Take turns...listen to me....You're making so much noise you're going to waken the baby."

The fire drill resulted in a game of follow the leader: out the window, across the roof, down the tree, around through the house, and up the stairs. The whole procedure was repeated again and again until Mama started to get a headache and the whole thing had to be stopped.

Mama warned the boys not to use the rope for escape unless there was no other way to get out of the house. That part of the fire drill procedure was not included in the practice as it was a rather dangerous exit. That rope was never used for its intended purpose, but Virl and Joe did not leave it idle. In later years it was out that window they made secret pilgrimages at night inspired, no doubt, by the writings of Mark Twain.

Laden with a mantled lantern and stolen canned fruit from the cellar, they would shinny down the rope, right in front of the window behind which Mama and Papa were sleeping, stealthily descending and tiptoeing away in the darkness to the far corner of the orchard. There they would uncover the lantern and eat the stolen food.

We girls were sworn to secrecy. All we could do was hope for their safe return. Grace and I would listen to the snores coming from downstairs, knowing full well that if Papa awoke, the boys would be severely punished for such a trick. While listening for the boys' return, we would get the giggles because Mama and Papa snored in different keys so the ensuing duet was both terrifying and amusing.

When we had finished the fire drill, I made the beds before going downstairs to help Mama with the morning work. She was sitting in the kitchen, nursing the baby and reading a book. The breakfast dishes were on the table and the hotcake griddle was pushed toward the back of the stove.

"Better run upstairs and close that window. The house will be full of flies. And before you do that," continued Mama, "put some more wood in the stove and some water on to heat for the dishes. I think the reservoir is nearly empty."

Mama went back to her reading. No matter how surrounded by the confusion of disorder and unfinished work, she seemed to find time to sandwich in moments for study. Her prolific reading gave her a fund of knowledge that provided our home with a walking encyclopedia. Her special interest was in the lives of historical characters about whom she could relate not only their heroic accomplishments, but also the sordid details of their private lives.

Mama had the ability to associate herself personally with people of the printed page. They became, for her, real flesh and blood with whom she could walk and talk. As she told us children about George Washington, I could feel the chill of a Pennsylvania winter. It was as if she had knelt in the snow with him there at Valley Forge and had heard him relate personal affairs unknown to the writers of history books.

History, although Mama's favorite subject, was not the only one about which she was well informed. There was always a fitting line of poetry to suit the occasion, be it Chaucer or Mother Goose, and regardless of subject at hand, Shakespeare seemed to have a quote worth repeating.

So it was, while the water needed to be heated and the dishes waited to be washed, something worthwhile was being read. No wonder the tasks of a household were humdrum to a mind that had hobnobbed with the best in literature and most significant in history.

Mama continued to read after the baby had stopped nursing. The tortoise shell hairpins were slipping from the loose coil of hair at the nape of her neck. Her dark hair, parted in the middle and drawn back in a simple knot, framed her face, which boasted a clear complexion and well-defined features. Papa's ultimatum, "No womenfolk in my house will ever wear face paint," was of little concern to Mama as her cheeks were highly colored, her lips a healthy crimson, and her grey-green eyes looked out from under heavy Welsh eyebrows that needed no accent of line or color.

"That there paint some women are daubin' theirsel's up with makes 'em look like an old hussy," was part of the sermon I would get once in awhile from Papa on the morality of women. "Land sakes, I've never seen a woman yet who cut her hair and ever amounted to nothin'. Believe you me, no girl of mine is agoin' to get her hair cut as long as I can he'p it. I ain't intendin' to raise no floozies."

While Mama was nursing the baby and doing a bit of reading, Papa and the new hired man were fixing the fence. Papa insisted the fences be built carefully with all the fence posts exactly the same distance apart. Papa seemed to have an obsession for orderliness. He spent untold hours doing unprofitable things to make the farm neat and tidy. Mama would often observe, "If your Papa would just pay more attention to the important things and forget all this straightening and tidying up we might get some place on this ranch. I can't see why he always has to have a hired man to 'elp him every time he turns around. You can't run a farm the way you do a grocery store."

That evening after supper when the chores were finished, Papa, Virl, and I went down to the creek to get some fish for breakfast. We had just started baiting our hooks when we heard Grace calling, "Wait for me! Wait for me!"

She was sitting down picking tar weed stickers out of her bare feet and crying, "Wait for me! Wait for me."

"Come on, Little Miss Muffet," called Papa, "we're waitin' for ye. Fishy, fishy in the brook, Grace'll ketch 'em with a hook, Mama'll fry 'em in the pan, Grace'll eat 'em like a man. Stop your snifflin'. You got to hold yer face jist right if you want to catch a fish. See that old Dolly Varden lookin' at you from that little riffle?" continued Papa, pointing to the water that rippled down over a rocky stretch.

Hawk Creek skirted the backyard and, all during the summer and autumn, it gave an invitation for fun and adventure to all who came close. Those who were affiliated with the Isaac Walton clan could not resist getting out the lines and hooks. Ours were often willow branches and bent pins. Eastern Brook and Dolly Varden lurked in the deep holes or flashed across the ripples.

Many fishermen from the neighboring towns often spent the better part of their weekends fishing along the creek. Most of them were very considerate but the few who trampled carelessly across the grain fields, left gates open, and obviously took more than the legal catch, made it necessary for Papa to post our farm with no trespassing without permission of the owner signs. Friendships suddenly blossomed with unknown anglers who formerly had not cared who owned the place.

While we were fishing, Papa noticed a gate had been left broken by some recent trespasser. While Grace and I were watching him fix the gate, a fisherman geared with the latest equipment strode across the field.

"You the owner of this place?" inquired the man.

"Yep, that's what I claim to be until I'm proven otherwise," replied Papa.

"Mighty fine farm here. I've always admired this place," remarked the stranger, patting his wicker creel. "You sure keep it looking well kept."

"That's my aim!" came Papa's curt reply, eyeing the fancy rod and reel.

"Well, I sure hope you aren't the kind of a farmer who thinks he owns the fish as well as the land. Wouldn't want to keep them all for yourself, would you? Mighty good fishing here. I've fished this place for eight years now and this is the first time I ever saw it all cluttered up with those no trespassing signs."

Papa's blue eyes were flashing. "Well, I'll tell you one thing, folks has got so careless about leaving gates open, and...."

"Well, I'm not to blame," interrupted the stranger, "for what other fishermen have been doing. Say, this is a right pert little girl you got here," he said, changing the subject and reaching over to give Grace's pigtails a jerk. "Guess I better be going if I'm planning to get my limit today. Glad to have met you. Probably be seeing you around."

Papa was a bit pale with anger and at a loss for words as the fisherman strode off toward the creek. "Well, I'll be corn swiggled. I never told that-what-ever-his-name-is-he could fish on this here place. What does them signs say? Without Permission of the Owner.... Why, I got half a notion to tell that trespassin' old cuss that he can't fish here. Who in tarnation does he think he is?"

After we had finished fixing the gate, Papa nailed it shut. As we walked back toward the creek, Papa said, "People sure like this here place. Didn't that trespassin' fisherman say I kept things lookin' right tidy?"

Chapter Six
North Carolina Grandparents
℘)Ↄ℞

*I*t was necessary to crawl under or through the barbed wire fence to take the short-cut up the hill to Grandpa's house. I was in a hurry and didn't want my brothers or sister to see me leaving. It was a tiresome trip when Joe went along. He was little and always got tired before we could get to the top of the hill. This time I was to borrow some of Grandma's lye soap and hurry right back.

When I left, the other children were wading in the creek and hunting for "penny winkles" to use for fish bait. The hired man called them periwinkles but Papa insisted they were "penny winkles." Grace and the boys were so busy searching on the rocks along the edge of the stream that they did not follow when Mama had called for me to come to the house. I am sure they thought I was going to have to do the dishes and they did not want any part of that tedious chore, unless Mama insisted.

I liked to go up the hill to Grandpa's house and especially when I was sneaking off without any of the little ones trailing after me. Grandpa and Grandma lived on a little farm. They had taken up a homestead within the boundaries of our ranch. Papa had said his ma and pa might as well have the land. It had been isolated with no access area, so he gave his folks a right-of-way through our place.

The road followed a little valley to get to the shelf of land where the homestead lay. The path we took when we walked was one made by the cows in the pasture, so we had to step precariously over the manure piles along the way. We would run barefooted along the trail to see who could miss the most cow pies and finish the race without what we called a "cut foot." The ones who had no "cuts" got to lick first from the salt block Papa kept for the cattle and horses. We often noticed that when the block was gone the cattle licked the bare spot on the hillside, which was dry and white.

"That salt lick," Papa explained, "ain't enough for the cattle. If they don't git enough salt they won't drink water and they'll bung up and die. Remember when old Roanie died last winter? Well, when I cut her open she was plum packed tight with straw. Those critters just won't drink water if they don't git enough salt. Now this here salt lick is natural salt acroppin' out on top of the ground. God's salt box, I guess you'd call it."

As I went along the trail I stopped at the salt lick and looked at the little grooves made by the animals' tongues in the hard alkaline hillside. Never once did I pass the salt lick without thinking of old Roanie. She had the kindest brown eyes and always stood still to be milked, even when her warty teats were cracked and sore. Papa bought Watkins salve for the cows' sore teats. It said on the can "good for man or beast." This recommendation puzzled me because I could not figure out any ailment for man that could be half so painful as a warty, cracked cow's teat.

As I studied the salt lick and thought again of old Roanie, I knelt down and licked the salty earth. If Watkins salve was good for man or beast, perhaps salt was, too. It tasted good but rather muddy. I did not want to get bunged up like old Roanie and bloat up and die, so I took several more licks and finally went on up the hill, hoping this would help prevent my untimely death.

Once on top of the hill I could see the smoke curling above the chimney. There must have been forty acres of benchland surrounding Grandpa's house. Piles of jackpines lay here and there about the uncultivated land. Grandpa's place was unfenced and only he and Papa and the county officials knew where the boundaries were. The only fence Grandpa had made was a crude split rail affair surrounding the buildings and providing protection from the cattle so Grandma could plant her everlasting flowers.

Grandma had a green thumb. I am sure she would have had some flowers growing in a short time even if she had been stranded on a desert without an oasis. Her flowers made a gay spot of this humble homestead. The bachelor buttons and little poppies had left the boundaries of the yard and were blooming far out over the benchland. There were larkspur and sweet William, nasturtiums and hollyhocks, baby breath and pansies, and many, many more. Each fall she gathered the seed and stored them for the spring planting. Little cloth sacks with drawstrings that formerly held Bull Durham tobacco served as containers for Grandma's seed supply.

As I walked on toward the house and past the bachelor buttons, I thought of the two Bull Durham sacks I had left on a rafter in the apple house where no one could find them. The reward for each sack was a piece of hard candy from a can Grandma kept in her big trunk. It had the faint taste of mothballs, but it was sweet and it was candy.

It was here among the scattered flowers that the trail across the benchland met the road, which came up through the little valley on the right. It was a narrow road and used only to bring the old folks back and forth for visits or to haul jackpines for fireplace kindling. We would ride along on the lumber wagon when Papa went to haul wood. The pine trees were pitchy and they left our hands black and sticky. Sometimes we would find pitch gum on the big trees at the edge of the woods. It was good to chew. If it was dark and hard it made good gum, but if it was too light and soft it was an unpleasant mess and almost an impossibility to part with.

As I neared the yard, I wished so much we could have more flowers at home instead of dogs and geese and chickens to break down each plant that struggled for existence. Mama raised only iris and hollyhocks and big sturdy rose bushes that defied any animal to come near. The iris were root bound and the hollyhocks seemed indestructible. Here at Grandma's I breathed in the fragrance and quietness of it all and I tried to imagine I was Heide on a Swiss mountainside.

The split rail fence around the yard had a turnstile for visitors to enter. The invention of the revolving door, no doubt, had its first inspiration in one of these old-time gates. Next to the turnstile was the wide gate which permitted wagons and sleighs to enter. It was on the bottom rail of this big gate that all the grandchildren weighed themselves when the family gathered at Grandpa's house. It was a very simple scale and gave only a relative answer to the weight question. There was a special stick for the measuring device, and this stick was held in a perpendicular position while the children took turns standing on the lowest rail and marking its positions on the stick. The one having the lowest mark on the stick weighed the most and the one with the highest mark weighed the least. After all, who cared how many pounds one weighed? The important point was who weighed the most.

This time there was no need to be weighed since there was no one to outweigh. I entered by the turnstile and walked toward the house. I could hear Grandpa reading the Bible aloud. We always stood still or walked very slowly when he read from the Bible. He liked the Psalms and read them again and again. As he neared the century mark of life, the Bible became more and more important to him.

I waited on the steps and, along with Grandpa's reading, repeated the last lines of the Twenty-third Psalm: "Surely goodness and mercy shall follow me all the days of my life and I will dwell in the house of the Lord forever."

Grandpa was slight and straight, a figure as clearly cut as his thinking. There was no pouchiness nor double chin, just a lean, wiry man with keen black eyes and lots of white hair.

His long white beard was always neatly combed. I was sure if Christ had been alive at that time, my grandpa, who resembled a picture of a prophet, could have been one of the disciples.

As he finished his Scripture reading, he spied me standing by the door.

"Come on in, Mollie, and set a spell. I haven't finished my devotions so you can he'p me sing a hymn."

I had no need to ask which one. I knew it would be "When the Roll is Called up Yonder." We sang all three verses and it was the third that seemed to speak of Grandpa's life. "Let us labor for the Master from the dawn till setting sun, let us talk of all His wondrous love and care; then when all of life is over, and our work on earth is done, and the roll is called up yonder, I'll be there."

After we'd finished the last chorus, Grandpa said, "You ain't singin' so pert this mornin'. Are you all tuckered out from climbin' the hill? It's a right smart piece twixt here and yer Pa's."

My throat was dry and I was thirsty. I had to be honest with Grandpa. I told him it wasn't the climbing that troubled my voice but the salt lick. That only reminded him of another reference in the Bible.

"Well, I do declare if that don't remind me of some more Scripture. Do you know where salt is first mentioned in God's Word?"

"It must have been Lot's wife turning to a pillar of salt," I quickly added.

"No, it was three centuries before the birth of Christ, here in the book of Job it says: 'Can an unsavory thing be eaten that is not seasoned with salt?'"

"I don't want anything to eat, I just got to get a drink of water."

"Run along, child, and git yerse'f a drink. Yer grandma is out in the back putterin' around the flowers. She'll be mighty glad to see you."

Just outside the back door I drank from a tin dipper the cool spring water that flowed from a two-sided, v-shaped wooden trough. This trough was used to bring water from a mountain spring several hundred feet down a slope to the back yard where it trickled into a moss-covered bucket and spilled over into little irrigation ditches for Grandma's ever-bloomin' flowers. The wooden trough was green with moss and the grass was well watered beneath where the water dripped through. Even though the trough was uncovered and used by the birds as a drinking fountain and a birdbath, the water was crystal clear and cool to drink. Occasionally the cows bumped sections of the trough apart but Grandpa proved to be a good maintenance man.

The July afternoon was hot but Grandma did not mind. She had spent most of her life beneath the North Carolina sun. She wore a sun bonnet and a long-sleeved dark dress that swished around her ankles. The sweet peas had to be picked every day to keep them blooming. As she placed an armload of them in a little wheel barrow, she groaned and rubbed her back. She was a raw-boned woman with a large nose and strong jaw. As I looked up into her face I noticed how wrinkled and weathered she looked. Wisps of thin grey hair hung beneath the sun bonnet. She was always busy, always seeing work that had to be done and eternally complaining about what everyone else should be doing. Grandma seemed to think there was always something to weed, something to patch, something to save from sudden loss. Papa said it was lucky Grandma got her second eyesight because she loved to make crazy quilts and darn socks. She had put away her glasses and could see to thread a fine needle.

As soon as Grandma saw me coming she called, "Fetch that bucket full of water with you and pour it on the yon side of these sweet peas. Sometimes I think I'd like to git shet of the whole lot of 'em. I'm plum nigh give out. I don't think I ever saw peas bloom like this back home. Ain't they a sight! But I reckon I'll be plantin' 'em agin next year. Don't dump that water all in one spot!"

"Grandma, Mama wants to borrow some soap," I explained as I poured the water carefully along the sweet peas.

"Lawse me, child. Seems as how all your ma does is wash and fix for you youngins. Think she'd want to put a tow sack on you and turn you loose."

I had to explain we needed some lye soap to bleach flour sacks. The store-bought soap just would not take out the lettering and the pictures. The flour we had been getting was from the Lincoln Flouring Mill and the picture on the sack was a life-sized head of Lincoln, which had been designed by some man from Peach, the little town that was our post office. Mama made my underwear from flour sacks and I was anxious the pictures be entirely bleached out and not like the bloomers I was wearing, with Lincoln's nose all wrinkled in the elastic waist band.

Grandma made the lye soap from grease she saved. Even the grease from the dishwater after the kettles and frying pans were washed was carefully skimmed and saved. The lye was made from wood ashes by a process that took a great deal of time and patience. The ashes were in a container through which water slowly dripped into a little pan below. Only a certain kind of wood was used to make the lye. It was all Grandma's secret formula. The resulting soap was good and it was a certain bleaching agent for the printed flour sacks.

The long years of the Civil War had left a never-to-be forgotten mark on Grandma's frugal soul. Those were days when frugality meant life itself. Skimping, saving, planning amidst the plunderings of a war torn land, she had lived alone with one small child, awaiting Grandpa's return from four years with the Confederate Army, served against his will and for a cause in which he did not believe. Grandma had never stopped working.

"Here's yer soap. Better be gittin' on down the hill. Yer ma's needin' yer he'p. Remember idleness is the Devil's workshop," admonished Grandma. As I waved goodbye and hurried along the path I felt like "a no-good, lazy youngin' who would never amount to nothin'."

The armful of sweet peas smelled good. I planned to put them high up on the sideboard where the little ones could not reach them. As I drank in the sweetness of the flowers, I remembered there would be goodness and mercy all the rest of my days, and I started running down the cow path, making sure I would not get a "cut foot."

Chapter Seven
Old Bill, the Hired Man
ഔ

*T*he walls of our home were well built but it was still possible for the noises to penetrate from the back room where Old Bill, Papa's most recent "hard hand," carried on his household chores. Mama felt he was quite obnoxious, and especially when his gastronomical difficulties had their obvious sound effects.

These muffled sounds were hilariously funny to us children, but our mirth was short-lived when Papa began his lecture on the respect due our elders.

"Now listen here, you youngins. Guess I'll jist halft to take ye down a notch or two. Now mind ye, I'll skin ye alive ef I ever kitch you payin' dis-respect to yer elders, no matter what they've a mind to do. I don't wanta hear tell of ye makin' fun of Old Bill. He ain't a very well man. He's ailin' and he jist can't he'p it."

"I think he's a hypochondriac," interrupted Mama, interceding for us children.

"I ain't akeerin' what perfession you might think he b'longs to, he's a sick man and these youngins is goin' to respect him."

"But, Papa," I added timidly, "Mama means one of those men that has to steal things."

"No, no, child," added Mama. "You're thinking of kleptomaniac, which is a person with a persistent impulse to steal. Now I think that Old Bill is a hypochondriac or a person who has imaginary illnesses. I'm sure he wouldn't steal anything."

While Mama was increasing our vocabulary Papa started to laugh, "Nope, Old Bill ain't one of them maniacs who would take nuthin' from nobody."

One evening not long after Papa had lectured us on the respect due our elders, we heard more than the usual amount of commotion coming from the back room. To the ordinary noises were added moans and groans and the sound of a body rolling across the floor, followed by some mournful cries for help. Papa went to investigate. We stood close to the inside door, which was locked for two-way privacy.

A coat hanging on the opposite doorknob kept us from seeing through the keyhole so, stealthily and carefully, we put our ears against the cracks around the door. Since the four of us were of assorted heights, we arranged ourselves so each had a good spot for listening. Papa would never have permitted this intrusion on privacy but Mama encouraged our eavesdropping. "Go ahead and listen. Maybe you'll get some first hand definitions of a hypochondriac."

Old Bill was rolling on the floor and groaning. We could hear Papa as he entered the back door. "What's ailin' ye, man? Do ye need a doctor?"

"Oh, I'm dyin', I tell you, I'm dyin'," he complained with more moans and groans. "Where do you hurt?"

"Hurt? Hell's fire, man! I'm dyin', I tell you! The old devil's got me in his clutches."

"Git up off'n that floor. You'll catch yer death-a-damn-folishment down there. Ain't likely yer agoin' to die. Git up and set here by the stove. Now, what was it ye et for supper?"

"Oh, I'm dyin', I tell you, I'm dyin'. All I had for supper was some buttermilk. Oh, I'm dyin'. When I started gettin' sick I took a big dose of sodee. I'm dyin' I tell you! I'm dyin'."

We all had to scatter away from the door as we heard Papa returning. He paid little heed to us as he stirred some liniment in a big glass of hot water. It was for external or internal use and was Papa's cure-all for any ailment.

Papa put the medicine bottle back in the corner cupboard at the end of the dining room. The top door on the cupboard was high above the reach of us children. Sometimes I was allowed to get things for Mama from the cupboard by standing on a chair, but unless given orders to do so, I was not to get into the cupboard.

On the few occasions I was sent to get some remedy, I always fumbled around long enough to look over the myriad of bottles, cans, tubes, and jars. Papa kept a stock of supplies on hand so he could doctor the family as well as the farm animals.

There was always a large bottle of castor oil, turpentine, liniment, camphor, cough syrup, a dark brown laxative, and Lydia Pinkham's Vegetable Compound. In smaller containers were pain pills, worm medicine, Nature's Remedy, Carbolic Acid, Golden Medical Discovery, and Dr. Pierce's Pleasant Pellets. I could figure out the labels on vaseline, boric acid, petrocarbo salve, mentholated ointment, and corn plasters. On the top shelf were sewing machine oil, de-lousing powder for chickens, Epsom salts, pine tar, senna leaves, and stock dip for ridding the animals of parasites.

As Papa went out the back door with the steaming drink, we children raced back to our listening posts. We snickered and giggled as we listened to Papa trying to persuade his patient to take his medicine.

"Now you swoller this. It'll either kill or cure ye and since yer wantin' to die, guess it twon't make no difference. Yer jist all swolled up, man, 'till yer 'bout to bust. That's all that's ailin' ye."

"Oh, I'm dyin'," moaned Old Bill. "The smell of that concoction makes me sicker. Take it away, I tell you."

"If yer aimin' fer me to he'p ye, ye better open yer mouth and swoller this, 'cause if you don't I'll git some soap suds and a hose and do a little irrigatin'."

After Papa's threat of more drastic treatment, we could hear Old Bill gulping and sputtering and complaining about the hot liniment.

"What are you trying to do? Set me on fire? I'm dyin', I tell you! That blamed stuff is hotter than the hinges of Hell. Oh, man! Now I am dyin'!"

After Papa had Old Bill quieted down for the night, he told us children, "Hit the hay now, you youngins. It's way past yer bedtime. Yer all stayin' up 'fraid yer agoin' to miss sumthin'." Then turning to me he added, "You shoulda been in bed hours ago, child. Yer eyes look like burnt holes in a blanket."

"Yes," added Mama, "we could all stand some more sleep. Sleep will cure both our physical and mental ailments. As Shakespeare so aptly put it, `Sleep, that knits up the ravell'd sleeve of care; the death of each day's life, sore labor's bath; balm of hurt minds; great nature's second course; chief nourisher in life's feast.'"

At the mention of the word feast, all of us, including Papa, immediately decided we were too hungry to go to bed, let alone to sleep. Mama cut some freshly baked bread, opened a jar of apple jelly and sent me to the cellar to bring up a pitcher of milk.

While we were eating we noticed Joe was asleep on his chair, his milk hardly touched and his hand clutching a half-eaten slice of bread.

"Hurry up, and finish eating and run on up to bed," urged Mama.

"Yep," said Papa.

> "To bed, to bed, said Sleepyhead,
> Wait awhile, said Slow,
> Put on the pot, said Greedygut,
> We'll eat before we go."

With Papa's homely verse ringing in our ears, we trailed up the stairs to bed.

The next day was Sunday. Papa had promised to take us to Uncle's house, which was across the creek on the adjoining farm. It was a little sidehill place adjacent to Papa's wheat field. Uncle and his wife had just bought a new phonograph and we were all invited to come over to see it and to hear it.

I often ran over to Uncle's house on an errand but seldom was there an occasion which merited an invitation for the whole family. This new phonograph was to be presented to us as a group. We could hardly wait until an appropriate time of day to make the visit. After we were washed, combed, brushed, and inspected, we walked across the fields to Uncle's house. We were welcomed at the door by Uncle's wife and we all marched in single file, in a very solemn manner. Mama and Papa stopped to chat a while at the door while we children filed into the living room and seated ourselves on the extra bedroom chairs that had been brought in for the afternoon.

When we were all assembled around the room, Uncle began his description of his new machine. He described in detail the mechanism of the thing and explained with what care it must be handled.

"This here handle on the side is fer windin' it up so you kin play it. A gramaphone ain't no plaything, so I don't want to see none of you youngins a tinkerin' with it. There's a little ol' needle here that is held in place on the end of this here arm and when this needle goes around this here record, there's goin' to be some powerful purty music a comin' outa this here horn. Now you all jist sit quiet like and I'll start with playin' 'Are You from Dixie?' It sure takes me back to ol' times down in North Carlinee."

Uncle stood close to the machine adjusting the speed to suit his mood. A tenor with a gravelly voice blurted out verse after verse. After we had heard "Are You from Dixie?" on the slow, medium, and fast speeds, Uncle turned the record over and announced we would now be favored with the rendering of "Don't Bite the Hand That's a Feeding You."

The second song was sung by the same mournful tenor. Uncle stood by in order to wind up the machine and start the record over again. He had only purchased one record to see if he would be pleased with the gramaphone's performance, so we were obliged to hear the same two songs repeated for our afternoon's entertainment, although each rendition was at a different speed.

While the tenor was warning us for the third time, in the slowest speed, not to bite the hand that is feeding you, my brother next to me decided to get up and make a dash for the outdoors. Mama reached out to stop him on the way by but he was too elusive. The rest of us sat ever so still as Uncle, looking very displeased, stopped the music and said, "Hmmrph!

You can sure see that youngin don't appreciated good music."

This unexpected dash for freedom on the part of my brother brought the afternoon's call to a sudden conclusion and we all stood, talked some more about the new gramaphone, and finally made our way outdoors. There were too many of us to stay for supper so Mama asked them to come over later and eat with us. Uncle said they would some other time because he wanted to get his chores done early so he could play the gramaphone some more before he went to bed.

Chapter Eight
Hawk Creek, God's Watering Trough

ജ൙ൕ

*H*awk Creek was the lifeline of our farm. Around this stream centered the many activities of our family life. It offered sandy wide stretches just right for wading, narrow deep holes better used for swimming, and rocky steep places with singing ripples, perfect for catching trout. At wide level places the water seemed to pause and the current to cease, waiting for me to skip a flat rock across the smooth surface and to count the ever-widening circles made by each touch of the bouncing, skipping stone.

As I searched the sandy shore for just one more round, flat rock, a killdeer fluttered across the way feigning a broken wing in an attempt to lure me from her nest. But I was wise to the ways of the killdeer and I did not follow her, but instead I searched among the sweet clover for her nesting place which was only a hollow in the ground. There I found buff-colored eggs, sharp at one end and covered with tiny black spots. I did not molest the private sanctuary of this noisy, faking killdeer who had fluttered away pretending to be lame and incapable of flight.

I looked at the bespeckled eggs and was concerned lest they became a lunchcounter treat for some egg-eating predator. These thoughts brought to mind the words of the poem I had learned in school.

To-whit, to-whit, to-whee.
Will you listen to me.
Who stole four eggs I laid,
In the nice nest I made?

I left the nest and hurried along down the stream to catch up with my brother. I was supposed to be helping him hunt for a lost pig when I became distracted by the antics of the mother killdeer.

We had found a pig missing from the pig lot that morning when we fed the animals. Since the men had gone out early to finish fixing the big pasture fence, my brother and I had been elected to do the morning chores.

After discovering a pig was missing, we fixed the escape hatch before other culprits might follow in their sister's footsteps, and then we went to look first in the most likely places.

The creek seemed the most logical spot to begin our search. Even if it had been out of our way, we would have gone there, for the stream had some magic lure to attract us to its banks. As we expected, we found the young sow wallowing in a cool, muddy spot not too far from our favorite swimming hole.

The problem then presented itself of getting the stupid animal to get up and out of the mud and to return to her proper quarters. We pushed and pulled and kicked her, which she apparently enjoyed as fond attentions. She grunted contentedly and wallowed deeper into the mud.

As I pulled on her ears I decided Mama was literally right when she said that "you cannot make a silk purse out of a sow's ear," at least not out of that sow's ear. When pulling the ears had no effect, we resorted to switching her with some willow branches, cut with a jackknife from the nearby creek bank. Apparently this did not meet with her approval, so she got up and took off toward the wheat field. Now this was the last place we would have wanted her to go. Papa's grain fields were off-limits for fishermen and livestock.

So then the chase began with the pig in the lead. We tore around through the grain in all directions. The pig was terribly confused. Just about the time we would catch up with her, she would let out a squeal and then take off in a different direction. After we had made a haphazard network of trails through the lush wheat field, we got the panting animal headed back toward the creek. This pig seemed to have a one-track mind, so when she met my brother head on, she did not swerve either to the right or left but dashed in between his legs, and within seconds he found himself, much to his surprise, astride the frantic pig, riding toward the mud wallow where he suddenly upended.

My brother was not one to be intimidated by a runaway pig. He came up out of the mud hanging onto the pig's hind leg and yelling for me to come to his assistance. I waded in and grabbed the other leg.

Between the two of us mud-bespattered youngsters, we wheelbarrowed that pig toward home. We had not gone very far when we saw Papa coming down the creek to meet us with a bucket in his hand. From external appearances, Papa could not discern, for sure, which one of us was the pig. As he came closer, he called out, "Let that critter go!" He rattled the bucket and, as we dropped the pig's hind legs, he let out a lusty hog call, "Pig! Pig, pig, pig! Soo-ee, soo-ee! Sooooo-eee!"

Papa turned and walked back toward home. The pig, like a well-trained puppy, tagged along after him, and we trudged along after the pig, feeling very much like the stupid Epaminondas, with a lesson dearly learned.

We looked at each other and Virl began to laugh. "You should see yourself—you look more like a baby dipped in tar than a girl. No wonder that pig was scared."

"You should see your own self," I replied. "You look more like a stick of licorice than anything I ever saw." We were both laughing as we raced up the sandy trail to the house.

The episode of the pig rescue gave us an opportunity to take time off from our morning's work for a much-needed swim. While swimming we swished our mud-drenched clothes through the water and then hung them to dry. The swimming hole was shoulder-deep for the oldest of us children, just right to have a lot of fun and to learn to dog paddle. Since we owned no bathing suits, we would array ourselves in most any variety of old clothes. The dresses would billow out like umbrellas when we went under the water and they would stick to our bodies when we came out dripping wet.

After swimming was over we would either stand shivering in the sunshine or cover one another with the warm sand and then have to jump back into the cool water for a last-minute swim.

While we were standing there shivering we began to discuss the baptismal service we had witnessed the week before. A minister, who had been holding some meetings in a nearby community, had been granted permission by Papa to use our swimming hole for baptismal services for a group of his new converts. We children had stood discreetly in the background and watched the whole proceedings with keen interest.

We decided to hold a baptismal service of our own, because Grandpa had told us we could be baptized in Hawk Creek some day. We sent Grace to the house to bring all the dolls and the teddy bear down to the creek. Virl was the pastor and I, the pastor's wife. I pretended to hold a book while he solemnly lowered each doll and teddy bear into and out of the water, saying what he thought were the proper words for such an occasion, "with justice and liberty for all!"

This did not seem enough of a ceremony for my brothers, so they caught the cats and brought them to the water. The cats were very unwilling converts and came up sputtering and trying desperately to escape. Since the dolls and the teddy bear had been fastened to the clothesline to dry, the boys thought the cats could be treated likewise. This proved to be a problem only for boys to solve, and solve it they did by tying the cats' tails together and hanging them over the line.

There is nothing more noisy or unnerving than a cat fight. The poor, wet, bedraggled felines squalled and scratched at each other and set up such a din of noise Mama came out and put an end to our services, which she explained were inhumane and sacrilegious.

Knowing I was usually held responsible for curbing such misdemeanors and desiring to escape a reprimand, I attempted to point the finger of suspicion at my brother. So I surreptitiously told Mama that Virl, the officiating clergy, was the instigator of the whole affair, thus trying to absolve myself.

Virl, although two years younger than I, stood his ground and in no uncertain terms let it be known I was a partner in this crime. Grace, who had been enticed into smuggling the dolls and teddy bear out of the house, stood innocently by while we two older children did all the talking. Joe, they younger culprit, chased off after the wet cats.

Mama, who was fond of animals, listened to both sides of the story and then scolded us all for participating in such an unkind act. By the time Mama returned to the house I felt as if I had taken part in some serious mob violence.

Virl was more concerned with my false accusations than with Mama's scolding. He glared at me. "Whose idea was this, anyway? Whatta ya got to always put the blame on me for? That's what I'd like to know. Scaredy cat! You ain't sproutin' no angel wings. Tattletail tit, your tongue should be split, and every little dog in town should have a little bit."

I decided to leave before Virl's anger at my injustice went beyond verbal expression. He was a big, healthy specimen of a boy and I had learned to respect his physical ability to cope with any offender, be it a sister or runaway pig.

As I went upstairs to change my clothes, I kept thinking of what Mama had said about us being sacrilegious and I felt pretty sure I had been condemned to Hell for our fiendish pranks. I knew my discipline would involve some kind of work.

When I came downstairs, Mama was at the creek picking chickens. She often scalded the chickens and then took them down by the creek to pick so the feathers might float down and away. We sat on the footbridge, holding the chicken by the feet and stripping off the wet smelly feathers, then meticulously picking out the pin feathers.

"I am glad that you're here. You finish picking these chickens. I've a lot to do tonight. Tomorrow is the Fourth of July and your papa has invited a lot of company to have a picnic here in our yard. He just got back from fixing fence awhile ago. He forgot to tell me we were going to have company until this afternoon. When I asked him what we were going to do for the Fourth he said, `Didn't I tell you we are havin' company?' I just wish he'd tell me when he asks folks to come. I don't have the house clean or anything cooked and now I'm going to have a house full of relatives and neighbors and hard-telling who else."

Mama had scalded six chickens and she evidently thought that was more than I could do alone, because she continued to pick feathers and talk after she had directed me to finish the job.

"Aren't these chickens big for this time of year? Lucky I set that first old hen that started to cluck. I always plan to have fryers by the Fourth. We can cook some potatoes tonight and boil a lot of eggs for a salad. I can't blame folks for wanting to come down here for the Fourth. The children can always play in the creek to keep cool. This stream always reminds me of Tennyson's Brook, `For men may come and men may go, but I go on forever'."

Mama took four of the chickens up to the house. I continued picking. The feathers were getting cold and the plucking was getting more difficult. Papa came down to the creek leading two of the mares. The horses lowered their heads, distended their nostrils, and drank long drinks of the cool water. Papa held the halter chains in his hand and waited patiently for the horses to finish drinking. He looked downstream and called to me, "Better hurry up with those there chickens. At the rate yer goin' it'll git dark on ye afore ye git through. Sure lucky I don't haf to pump water fer these thirsty old mares. It ain't everybody's got a crik in his own backyard. It comes in mighty handy like, God's watern' trough—that's what I calls it."

As Papa went back to the barn leading the two mares, he started whistling Yankee Doodle. I knew he was happy and he must be thinking of tomorrow and the Fourth of July.

Chapter Nine
Fourth of July Celebration
ಬಿಂಬ

*I*mmediately following each annual Fourth of July picnic, which was held in our front yard, Mama would irrevocably cancel all future repetitions of the affair. The next summer Papa, entirely on his own, would invariably revive the custom and dispatch the invitations in person. The machinery of preparation would go into gear about July third when Papa would surprisingly announce, "We're gonna have company tomorree. We're gonna celebrate right here at home. I ain't gonna go galavantin' around the country somewhere jist to celebrate with a bunch of roughnecks.

"Might as well have a doin's right here in our own front yard. I jist ain't a-hankerin' to drive a team on the road these days with those honkin' jitneys. A man's liable to have a runaway. We'll do our own whoopin' it up right here t'home."

With that detailed announcement from Papa, Mama would go into her annual dither, "Why on earth don't you tell a person you are going to invite people to come here? You know good and well I don't have the house in order or the washing done. Yesterday when you went to town you expected the children and me to weed the potato patch. I told you last year I have more than I can do without preparing a dinner for every Tom, Dick, and Harry you take a notion to invite to a picnic."

"Now, now," said Papa. "Don't go gittin' yer dander up. Can't a man ask a few people onc't a year for a meal in his own front yard? No need to go to any fuss. I got some farworks hid away in my trunk. These youngins is goin' to have a little fun. Down South, 'bout the only time ye ever see farcrackers is at Christmas time. These youngins shouldn't miss havin' some farworks."

The morning of the Fourth was clear and sunny. Neighbors and relatives began to arrive much too early to suit Mama, who needed every extra minute to get things in a presentable condition. I was kept busier than the director of a three-ring circus. Virl, the family mechanic and inventor, was assigned the job of fixing the broken ice cream freezer, while Grace was to play with Joe and try to see he stay out of mischief and keep his clothes clean. Baby John, who had only recently started to toddle around, was left in his crib with an assortment of playthings.

Mama was frying chicken in the hot kitchen while Papa was out in the front yard making the lemonade. The lemonade was made in a five-gallon crock, which was dull grey with a big number five on the side and a row of blue fleur-de-lis around the top. Papa stirred the mixture with a long-handled wooden spoon, badly worn from years of stirring. He tasted, added more sugar, stirred again, and finally decided it needed more lemons. The lemons were rolled under the palm of his hand until they were soft and warm. The juice was squeezed from the neatly cut halves and the remaining rinds were sliced thin and added to float on the surface of the lemonade.

Chunks of ice were the last ingredient. They had been unearthed from a sawdust pile at a neighbor's ice house which contained the remains of last winter's ice, which had been cut from the frozen creek during the subzero weather of late January.

Our place could boast of most every type building known to a farm except an ice house. Each year Papa talked of building one but it never got done in time for the January freeze, so each Fourth some invited guest brought the ice for the lemonade. There was always the discussion of the purity of frozen crik water but it was soon forgotten when the lemonade was passed around.

Lemonade was Papa's master concoction. As a group gathered around to watch the proceedings of the lemonade making Papa, extrovert that he was, put on quite a show of his expertise while he chanted, "Lemonade, made in the shade, stirred by the fingers of a handsome old maid."

By that time Virl had the ice cream freezer working. He was truly mechanical by nature and could fix broken farm equipment that often baffled the hired men and Papa. He had a knack of understanding the intricate parts of machinery and was chief repairman for the farm.

Fixing the ice cream freezer proved to be a simple task. Virl soon had the crank turning the paddles inside the cream-filled cylinder which was surrounded by a mixture of coarse salt and chipped ice. His sturdy arm kept the freezer going at a rapid pace, while his tousled blonde hair flopped back and forth with each turn of the crank.

The tables, made of boards put across sawhorses, were set under the apple trees. As the people began arriving, bowls and pans of food, carefully covered to keep out the flies and yellow jackets, were placed on the tables. Family baskets of dishes and silverware were tucked under the table, out of reach of dogs and cats.

The first to arrive were the Edwards, a family Papa had quite a time convincing Mama he had not invited. Old Man Edwards had once been one of Papa's "hard men." They had two children and lived in a little house Papa had located for them as temporary living quarters many months ago.

The Edwards family, incidentally, came to call the morning of the picnic. Since they lived quite close, they had walked and were hot and tired. They sat like lumps on the chairs we had carried out from every room in the house and asked for lemonade before Papa had pronounced it ready for drinking.

While nearly all the guests contributed something toward the picnic, the Edwards family brought nothing but their appetites. They had had a few pet chickens at home but they were not for cooking. All of their chickens were rather privileged characters, being granted permission to come into the house anytime they so desired. The old hens would perch about the room, fluff their feathers, and blink their eyes. The chickens were introduced to any visitors who came to call. "This is Fluffy Legs. Hop down, old girl, and give the man a chair. That's Old Ruffle Neck on the wood box. She doesn't like visitors. The clothes basket is a good nestin' place for Old Wry Tail. She started clucking yesterday."

Old Man Edwards had worked for Papa a year ago during the busy season, but had worked very little since. He was a raw-boned hulk of a man with a tremendous appetite. With each meal he drank hot water in which he dissolved a green powdery mixture of herbs, cathartic in nature. He claimed this practice was necessary due to the severe illnesses he had survived.

He was quite the teller of tall tales, claiming not only to have survived rare ailments, but had experienced terrible accidents, performed wondrous feats of strength and skill, and had maintained his claim of sanity while enduring the mental cruelty of the worse set of in-laws of any man on the face of this earth. He termed his wife, Old Lady Edwards, in-law number one.

Old Man Edwards's family were often in dire need of food. Mama once offered them some of the small potatoes we had at harvest time, saying, "I know these potatoes are small but they are better than nothing."

Old Lady Edwards was quite rebuffed. "If we can't have bettern' nothin', we don't want nothin'." But they had come to call on the Fourth of July hoping to get something better than nothing.

Other neighbors and relatives were soon cluttering up the scene. Everyone was talking at once. Grandpa found a comfortable, shady spot, hooked his cane over the arm of the chair, and leaned back to doze for awhile. Perhaps if he closed his eyes he could shut out some of the confusion. His part in the picnic would come later when the blessing was invoked on the accumulation of vittles. Grandpa gave thanks for everything, but especially for food and raiment.

Both grandmas were in the house helping and confusing Mama. Her mother insisted there should be some fresh tangle-foot put out and immediately took a dish towel and started shooing some buzzing flies out of the room, while Papa's mother went to the stove and stirred and turned all the food, tasting each kettle full with the same spoon.

Our Rhode Island Red rooster bade them welcome by coming up on the back porch and crowing through the broken screen door. I thought perhaps he was saying farewell to his departed wives of the frying pan, but my grandmas felt differently.

Mama's mother had a Welsh superstition, no matter what the occasion. "Well, listen to the old fellow, would you! Sounds as if we're going to 'ave some more company."

"Hmmmph! The dog's foot!" grunted Papa's mother. "I can't he'p but think it sounds as if the back fence needs fixin'."

Cousin Hank could not be with us for the Fourth. He was one of Papa's distant relatives who usually was included on the invitation list, a peg-legged old bachelor who liked nothing better than a picnic.

"Cousin Hank is one of those shirt-tail relations," said Papa, "that I can't figger out for more than a kissin' cousin who ain't been kissed for quite a spell."

Cousin Hank did "peddlin'" for a living. He was sort of a retailer of farm produce, going from house to house selling whatever people might buy. But Cousin Hank had a sideline that was more lucrative than the usual products he was legally peddling.

This was during the time of the "dry" years in our country, so Cousin Hank contributed to the alleviation of that dryness by dispensing a home-produced commodity much in demand by many of his favorite customers.

Just before the Fourth of July, Cousin Hank had thoroughly tested his home product and inadvertently attempted to gain a new customer who was detailed to the enforcement of the law. Cousin Hank's sideline had forcibly folded up. Although there was a hush-hush about the whole incident, my Welsh grandma—who felt we had been scandalized—said, "Whatever comes over the Devil's back will go back under 'is belly." My inquisitive ears had heard enough bits of conversation to know it was for no good reason Hank was absent from the picnic.

"Where's that pot-bellied cousin of yours?" inquired our neighbor. "Old Hank's usually the first one out for a celebration. He's the one who can't keep his cotton-pickin' fingers off the chicken platter. Haven't seen him around here yet."

"Nope, he won't likely be showin' up today," replied Papa. "Cousin Hank jist couldn't see his way clear to git here. He's a mite under the weather. Better have another glass of lemonade." I noticed Papa filled Mr. Davidson's glass from the old aluminum pitcher which was reserved for just the two of them.

"It wouldn't be like the Fourth without drinking some of your lemonade. Family men like us has got to stay sober. Here's to yer health," laughed Mr. Davidson, holding his jelly glass of lemonade high above his head. "Guess we're both holdin' up pretty well. I'm one ahead of you, though, got a half-dozen mouths to feed, that's six pair of legs, not countin' my old ladies', under this man's table," he finished, pounding himself on the chest and strutting about as if to show off his youthfulness.

"Now don't go pattin' yerse'f on the chest too soon, Davidson. I'm goin' to even that score fer very long. Jest don't be too surprised when you hear what Santa Claus is goin' to be leavin' on our doorstep come Christmas time."

"Well, I'll be," said Davidson, faking a look of surprise. "Gimme another drink of that lemonade." Looking around to see who might be listening before continuing with his remarks, he altered his tone of conversation to include the children who were drooling at the thought of a cool drink. "Well, well! Seems we have a whole line of intruders waitin' to knuckle in on this punch bowl."

Papa snapped to attention, saluted the drooling faces and empty jelly glasses, ordered the straggling youngsters to "Line up over at the far end of the yard. Let's have a Fourth of July parade. You oughta know how this here marchin' should be done," he added, turning to Grandpa. "You marched through four years of Civil War. Why don't you put 'em through their paces, Pa?"

"Nope," came back Grandpa, with his brown eyes flashing. "I never give no orders to no man, and I ain't intendin' to start now. General, this is yer army, run it any way ye see fit. Jist don't march 'em into enemy territory. I'se real comfortable. I'd jist like to set here for a spell and review the troops."

Papa insisted everyone get in the line up, with the tallest at one end and shortest at the other. Davidson's oldest daughter, Dorothy, was at the head of the line with me standing next. Both of us girls felt we were too old for this kind of an exhibit, but Papa declared an all out draft, and Papa's orders were not to be tampered with, especially in the presence of company where he seemed to like to exercise his unmitigated authority and expected nothing less than absolute obedience.

The line up included five Davidsons, two Edwards, and four from the home camp.

"Hattention!" shouted Papa, waving the big wooden spoon like a saber in the sunlight, "Mark time! Left, left, left, right, left. Halt! Looks like most of ye have two left feet. About face! To the rear, march!" With that final command there was utter confusion.

"Git back, the hull lot of ye. Let's try it single file. Mollie, you better git in the lead. Dorothy can foller you. Hattention! Forward, march! Hep. Hep. Hay foot, straw foot, belly full of bean soup. Hep. Hep. Hep John Kelly with an Injun rubber belly. Hep! Hep!"

No majorette on a college gridiron ever strutted before a more appreciative audience than I did that July day as I led that motley group like the Pied Piper of Hamelin. We zigzagged among the apple trees, around the tables, and right through Grandpa's enemy territory, carried along by the momentum of Papa's cadence.

Mama and the other womenfolk deserted the kitchen and stood on the porch, potholders in hand, dishtowels across the shoulders, applauding and laughing at Papa's drill team.

Old Lady Edwards, who was above the menial tasks of a holiday kitchen, sat placidly in the shade of the tree where she had first seated herself upon arrival. She was ignored by the other women who knew well her role of assumed class distinction. Mama's mother whispered to the others, "Well, I see our majesty, Lady H'Edwards, is still stuck to 'er throne."

Old Man Edwards, who was disgruntled not only at the delay of the dinner but also at the performance of his obviously clumsy offspring, called out to Papa, "Listen here, John Kelly, how kin ye expect those two youngins of mine to know which is their left foot? Why, I ain't been able to learn 'em which one is their right foot, yet."

"Hmmph!" grunted Papa's mother, going back into the kitchen. "Some folks ain't got the sense God promised a goose."

Papa, who was enjoying his self-appointed job as master of ceremonies, began to sense the impatience of growing appetites so, as he gave each member of his marching unit a glass of lemonade, he reminded us, "Now don't ye go trapesin' off somewhere; we're goin' be eatin' drekly."

It was not long until Papa was calling, "Soup's on! Come and get it!" There was much juggling of chairs and general discussion as to where we should sit so each smaller child would be near someone who could be of assistance. Mama and Mrs. Davidson insisted they eat later. They said they were not very hungry and someone had to wait on the table. Both grandmas wanted to wait but were soon urged into chairs with the rest of us. Old Man Edwards was the first one to get a chair, soon followed by Lady Edwards, who elbowed in close to Grandpa at the head of the table. Dorothy and I managed to sit fairly close together with two smaller ones between us and one on each side.

We all bowed our heads and Grandpa waited in silence. As long as there was whispering or audible wiggling, Grandpa waited. In that silence there descended a peacefulness over us all, a quietness that meant even more than the words to follow. Grandpa asked forgiveness for all the things we had done and for a lot of things we had never thought of doing. He gave thanks, unlimited thanks, and enumerated all he was thankful for.

While Grandpa was praying, I half-opened my eyes and looked at the platter of chicken in front of my plate. I spied a gizzard and planned to get it before Virl did. Looking just above the chicken, Virl's eyes, from across the table, looked into mine. There was a look of a silent wager, a wager that had its inception the day we both discovered a chicken has only one gizzard. Today there should be six gizzards and I could see only one.

Grandpa finished the blessing and his "Amen" was the downbeat for my brother and me to get that gizzard and settle the wager. There were looks of surprise from both of us as we each retrieved a gizzard. We had something for which we cared very little, now that neither of us were left empty-handed. Just a tough, grisly, morsel that had once been a chicken's food grinder, to be eaten greedily if the wager was won, to make the loser drool at the sight of the delicious dainty.

Our breach of etiquette went unnoticed as Old Bill came from behind the house, clearing his throat, hitching up his trousers, and eyeing the lot of us like a sadly neglected old man. In the bustle of the picnic preparations, our hired man had been slighted by the family. He had not been given an invitation, a personal invitation to the Fourth of July picnic.

"Git up, Joe, and give Bill yer chair," said Papa, as if there was nothing unusual about Old Bill's dramatic approach. "It don't hurt ye to stand while ye eat. You can hold more that way. Come on, Bill, there's always room for one more. Squeeze in there by Ma. She ain't gonna mind a good-lookin' young man like you settin' by her."

Old Bill, the connoisseur, sat down without further comment. It was evident there were times when he could eat other people's cooking.

The rest of the picnic was a series of passing food and insisting the little ones clean up their plates. Mama kept shooing the flies and yellow jackets away from the table by swishing a dishtowel back and forth above our heads.

"Now just sit still. Those yellow jackets won't bite if you don't swat at them," instructed Mama, just as Joe began to cry. His lower lip was beginning to swell and it was evident one yellow jacket was trying to share his watermelon. This incident added a note of excitement to the picnic, with each adult advising his favorite remedy for bee stings. They suggested ice, salt, soda, and even tobacco juice.

After Mama finished doctoring Joe's swollen face, she opened the ice cream freezer. All of the children wanted to have the dasher, with each one insisting it was his turn.

"Can't you wait until I get it out of the ice cream?" said Mama, tugging at the dasher with the assistance of Mrs. Davidson.

"It's my turn! I want it this time! I never have had a turn!" came the chorus of voices from all sides of the table.

"Quiet down. Let's settle this peaceably," added Mama, starting a rhyme as she pointed in turn to each child present. "Eenie, meenie, minie, moe. Catch a Welshman by the toe. If he hollers, let him go. O-U-T spells out goes he."

A silence fell over the children as they watched Mama's finger pointing to the Edwards boy. She lifted the dripping dasher over to his plate. We watched his tongue slide along the creamy blades and the melting ice cream drip down his chin. The ice cream from the freezer could never taste that good. Licking the dasher was a special way of celebrating the Fourth of July.

Chapter Ten
The Swimming Hole

ഇര

*T*he longest hour of that Fourth of July day was the one between the last mouthful of food and that first step into the cool waters of our favorite swimming hole. Mama insisted every child wait the full sixty minutes after eating before going into the creek to swim. Her warnings indicated even the fifty-ninth minute could hold its implications of imminent tragedy. Next to her fear of fire was Mama's fear of water. At swimming time she could think of nothing comparable to our fire drill but she could enforce the minimum sixty-minute waiting period between food and water.

When Mama had finished announcing the rule for all swimmers to observe, Papa sang out, "Mama, Mama, may I swim? Yes, my darlin' daughter. Hang your clothes upon a bush, but don't go near the water."

With that comment, Mama said no more, but the children, by a majority voice, had the pie and cake postponed until later in the day, thus initiating the hour-long waiting interval.

"I reckon," said Papa, "you all better wait until tomorree. You've all et so much now, ya got chicken stickin' out yer ears."

Most of the intervening hour was spent outfitting each child in the least he could wear and get by Grandpa without being classified as a heathen or a savage. Finally the long wait was over and the scantily clad youngsters stepped from their little piles of clothing left on the bedroom floors and headed for the water.

Virl was in the lead. He was an excellent swimmer. His physical accomplishments seemed to be inherent. Close behind him was Grace who, although two years younger and much smaller, was his brave imitator, imitations which were often to get her into some precarious circumstances from which she must be rescued. Grace was little and agile and by sheer determination could fairly well keep up with her big brother in some of his daring accomplishments. At least close enough to be heard calling, "Wait for me!"

I came along with the rest of the children. I was to be responsible for their survival.

Before Virl reached the creek, he saw two fishermen vying for the best spot to cast their hooks. It was quite apparent these two men were novices in the art of fishing. In the heat of the July afternoon it was impossible to catch fish in the sunny open spots even with a barbecued angle worm for a lure. The fish were conspicuous by their absence. They were off in the cool shadows of the watercress or suspended listlessly in the shelter of a bank and no tempting tidbit at the tip of the nose could elicit the least bit of interest. It was just no time for fishing.

With the approach of us children, the men made known their piscatorial rights on the premises.

"Get out of here. Can't you see we're fishing?"

Virl, who was accustomed to strangers along the creek, dashed by the men and landed cannon-ball style in the middle of the deep water. To avoid the inevitable barrage of remarks from the angry fishermen, I followed Virl into the creek. The visiting children were not so brave. They cautiously came in step by step and would not enter the water until we splashed on ahead of them, showing them it was fun and not to be feared.

The men, seeing the impossibility of coping with the children, went on down the stream, muttering, "This younger generation shows no respect for its elders."

The swimming hole was soon churned to a frothy turbulence by the splashing, shouting crowd. The older children took turns giving the younger ones piggyback rides through the deep water. Dorothy, who did not know how to dog paddle let alone swim, was reluctant to enter into the fun. She was afraid of the water and disliked the idea of getting wet above her knees. As she edged her way into the creek, she stepped into a hole that had a sudden drop-off. She came up sputtering and stumbling forward into even deeper water.

We were all yelling warnings which went unheeded as she frantically struggled to stay afloat. Finally I was able to get to her side and attempt to help her. As I reached out to take her arm, she turned toward me and in one desperate lunge, grabbed me about the neck and plummeted me to the bottom.

I pushed and pulled at her arms, which gripped my neck like a vise. I was soon fighting for my life, coming up and going down under with Dorothy's arms tight around me. We bobbed about like two giant puppets with no one at the controls. Virl came to my assistance. Somehow he was able to get us both to shallow water. With our feet on the sandy footing, we staggered out to the shore. Dorothy started crying and I folded up like a wet sheet, crumpling to the ground.

Moments later, I looked up to see Papa bending over, rolling me from side to side and calling my name. The wet, shivering children made a semi-circle about us. Dorothy pulled at her father's sleeve and sobbed convulsively, "I thought I was going to drown."

Mr. Davidson, with his arm about his frightened daughter, was shouting, "I wouldn't raise my family along this blamed creek if you gave it to me."

Papa helped me to a sitting position. My throat hurt, there was a stinging sensation in my nose, and it was hard to breathe.

"She wouldn't let loose of me," I gulped as I brushed the wet hair back from my face.

"Now yer all right, sister," Papa reassured me. "You jist strangled a bit. Yer agoin' to find out you can't drink that old crik dry. Come on, you youngins, let's git on some dry clothes. Soon as that ice cream's gone, we're agoin' to have some farworks that'll make ye all come to."

As we walked toward the house, Dorothy came quickly to my side. She was pale and trembling. Virl was on the other side, asking, "Shall we make a cat-saddle and carry you?" The younger children had dashed on ahead of us to tell of the dramatic incident to the women who had missed it all. Through the clatter of dish washing, the hubbub at the swimming hole had gone unnoticed.

At the first words about the incident, Mama rushed out the door and began admonishing me, "I've warned you children about the chance of drowning in that deep water."

For the first time I began to realize perhaps Mama's fears were not completely unfounded. Her warnings of possible dangers had never been taken too seriously because Papa's "Go ahead and try" canceled out Mama's "Be carefuls." For every ounce of Mama's caution, Papa had a pound of assurance. My parents' opposing convictions about facing unusual situations had a subtle way of preparing me to hold caution in one hand while I reached for adventure with the other.

When our clothes were changed, we filtered out of the house and reassembled at the picnic table. Mama made some coffee and cut the cakes. The ice cream freezer was reopened and the children were soon asking for seconds.

Mr. Davidson continued to berate the stream of water that meant so much to our family. Old Man Edwards interrupted to tell of the many times he had miraculously saved people from drowning. Through it all Mama and Papa remained quiet. They finished serving the desserts and made ready for the fireworks. Mama reminded us of the dangers wrapped up in those innocent-looking oriental noisemakers. "I sometimes wish," she said, "that we'd never heard of the things."

The proving grounds for the big display was on the sand bar at the back of the house so there would be less danger of setting a fire with the smoldering remains of a rocket or firecracker.

Papa personally supervised the firing of the more spectacular fireworks. The rest of us stood or sat on the back porch, which provided a grandstand view of the backyard which sloped down to the sand bar and on to the creek. Mama discussed the use of asbestos suits often worn by professionals while Papa gleefully sent the big rockets skyward.

Old Bill, the hired man, who had gone to his room for an afternoon snooze, bounded out of bed at the sound of the first exploding fireworks, stuck his head out the door, and growled, "Hell's fire, man, what's goin' on out here?"

When the supply of big fireworks was exhausted there were glowing sparklers that glistened and sputtered as they were twirled and twisted through the twilight air. There remained a red-hot wire which afforded a sizzling plop when it hit the water beyond the sand.

Following the sparklers were firecrackers of various sizes. Virl was permitted to put some big ones under a tin can to make a special explosion. Every child was allowed to set off at least one firecracker and nearly everyone came through unscathed. There were a few minor burns which required Mama's first aid from the medicine chest in the corner cupboard.

The fireworks depleted, the visitors found little reason to tarry longer. Remainders of the picnic were tucked into baskets, goodbyes were said, and the neighbors were on their way to do their evening chores.

Our grandparents stayed for a while longer after the crowd was gone. The leftover food was spread on the kitchen table for a late supper. Papa's mother said, "It's mighty good not to have to git supper from the stump out."

Even though everyone complained of a lack of appetite, the cold chicken, salad, and cake suddenly disappeared. Our Welsh grandma made the tea. When it was poured, little sticks were floating on top of some of the cups. "Now, those were visitors," said Grandma. "If they are long, the visitors will be tall and if they are short, the visitors will probably be women or children. I could be tellin' your fortunes when the cups are h'empty."

Little bubbles danced on the surface of the tea as the sugar sank to the bottom. Catching and drinking these little bubbles of good fortune before they touched the edge or burst in midair, was regarded by the Welsh as a good omen. Be it riches or good luck, when Papa heard the bubbles echoing back as healthy belches, he would remark, "I sure do hate to be laughin' up my sleeve, but it sounds mighty like yer good fortune is kinda back farin', ain't it?"

The conversation at the table turned to the swimming episode. I was again lectured by both parents and grandparents about the rules of water safety. There were detailed accounts of drownings and near-drownings.

Grandpa, with over ninety years of life behind him, felt the good Lord had kept him afloat on many occasions. "Why I been spared all these years is not fer me to be sayin'."

Grandpa's voice was getting husky and the tears were filling his eyes. He got up from his chair, and reaching for his cane, said, "I reckon, Ma, we better be goin' on up home."

"Don't git in no hurry," remarked Papa. "I'll hitch up the team and run ya up the hill in a little while."

"You know," said Grandma, "when Pa gits to talkin', none of the rest of us kin get a word in edgewise."

"Papa's got the horses ready to go, Grandma," interrupted Virl. "He wants you and Grandpa to come on before it gets any darker outside."

We hated to see Grandma and Grandpa leave. Their stories of by-gone days fascinated us. It had been an eventful Fourth of July and bedtime came all too soon.

While Papa was taking his folks home, our Welsh grandma, who was going to stay all night, helped the little boys get ready for bed. She insisted we all have our toenails trimmed, a task Mama often neglected. We were tired and not concerned about toenails, but Grandma was not to be deterred. She went after toes like a blacksmith shoeing a colt.

Grandma said Tuesday was a lucky day for nail trimming. If it had been Friday we would have to have gone untrimmed. To prove her philosophy of the pedicure, she quoted an old rhyme,

"Cut them on Monday, cut them for health;
Cut them on Tuesday, cut them for wealth;
Cut them on Wednesday, cut them for news;
Cut them on Thursday, a pair of new shoes;
Cut them on Friday, cut them for sorrow;
Cut them on Saturday, true love tomorrow;
But the man had better never been born
Than to have his nails on Sabbath shorn."

Each time Grandma stayed over night at our house, we each went to bed a little cleaner, a little neater, and a little more learned in the ways of superstitions.

Chapter Eleven
Grandpa Recalls the Civil War

ഇൻൽ

*T*he weather had become extremely warm in the days following the Fourth of July. This unusually hot weather had caused Grandpa and Grandma to plan to move back to Yakima earlier than usual. The little homestead house was not well insulated and they were eager to get back to the city where they usually spent the winters.

Last week Grandma had said, "It gits mighty tiresome having yer Pa haulin' us back and forth in the buggy. Now down in Yakima we have two sons' and three daughters' families to tote us around. They all have cars. I's told you about the little furnished home we git to live in each winter. Our older boy keeps it for us and it is right next to his'n."

"But we don't want you and Grandpa to leave," said Grace. "We like you and we like the candy you keep in your trunk."

"Now you don't to worryin', child. We'll be back come springtime cause this here Hawk Creek Canyon reminds us of North Carolinee, and besides, yer ma and pa need our he'p."

Early one day when we had the farm chores done, Papa said, "You three youngins go up to Ma and Pa's and see if you can he'p 'em pack some of their belongin's. You know we leave all the furniture so it will be ready when they come back next spring. Day after tomorree Uncle and me is taken 'em to Davenport to board the train for Yakima."

When Grace, Virl, and I got to Grandpa's homestead house, he was standing at the door, he motioned for us to be quiet because Grandma was resting. He told us to go around the house to the backyard where we could sit in the shade.

"Yer grandma is all tuckered out. I'se jist been sittin', cogitatin', and askin' the good Lord to take care of us."

"Papa told us to come up here to help you and Grandma get things packed. Day after tomorrow Uncle and Papa are going to take you to the train in Davenport," said Virl. "Now what do you want us to do?"

"Well, young man, I tell ye, we got the packin' all done but since you's so handy fixen' things I'd sure appreciate it if you'd go up along the waterin' trough and fix it where the cattle or deer has knocked it off the props. The girls can set here with me 'till Ma wakes up."

Grandpa and I sat there while Virl went to fix the trough and Grace chased off after a butterfly. I broke the silence when I commented, "You know, Grandpa, I thought I was going to drown on the Fourth of July when Dorothy held me under the water."

"I recollect I'll never fergit one afternoon when drownin' could a happened mighty easy. It was during' the war. It was powerful hot that day and we'd been farin' away since dawn. I got separated from all the men who was alivin'.

"I was gittin' mighty thirsty when I come to a stream. That water shore looked good. I knelt down and had a drink, using my hands for a cup. When I'se washin' my sweaty face, my cap fell into the water and started floatin' away down stream.

"Jist about that time a bullet hit a rock and ricocheted off in my direction. I'se reachin' out fer my cap jist in time to ketch that there bullet right along the top my scalp.

"Guess it sorta stunned me. Anyway I fell forward into that water and I never did git my cap. You all know right well that I never drowned, cause I'm settin' right here to tell ye about it.

"Yep, I'se saved from drownin' all right, but that was a mighty good clip I got clean along the center my noggin. That old Union bullet outlined a Mason Dixon line drekly down the center of my head. It give me a right natural part."

Grandpa chuckled as he went on with his story. "I splashed that cut with some water and made a compress of some grass and leaves. Then I jist lay back and closed my eyes. Never did that meadder grass feel so good.

"While I'se layin' there gittin' my faculties back, the words of David's Psalm came to me jist as clear as crystal. `He maketh me to lie down in green pastures, He leadeth me beside the still waters, He restoreth my soul.' With those there words on my lips, I got up and stumbled across the field. That night I bedded down with my own men.

"The battle was over and some of the Union boys was a-campin' right across a holler from where we was. They kept a yellin' across at us that evenin'. My head was ahurtin' so I couldn't sleep. I remember some loud mouth a-yellin', `Don't you rebels want some grease for your backsides so you'se can slide back into the Union?'"

"Was that the night General Jackson was shot?" I asked, hoping Grandpa would go on with his stories.

"Nope, that twarn't the night. It was drekly after that. Jist about dusk one evening that the general was wounded by one of his own men. He told us to shoot first and then ask questions. We never knowed he was a-coming into camp.

"Yep, some of us was a-gittin' supper. That was at Chancellorsville in the summer of '63, somewhere about the first of May, I reckon. It musta been powerful late to be cookin' supper, cause it was gittin' dark as I remember. That was the day General Howard got a big surprise from us. They was a retreatin' in all directions.

"Things had quieted down a little when someone yelled, `Yankee Cavalry'. There was a lot of shootin' and the next thing I knowed the general's horse, `Little Sorrel`, was a-runnin' right at us, all saddled and bridled. I knew right well somethin' was wrong.

"One of the men caught the horse. There was blood on the saddle and the horse was a-quiverin' all over, riderless and panicky.

"Drekly there was a young fella come runnin' up sayin' the general was shot in the arm. It was purty awful the way us men felt when we heard Stonewall was wounded. We all fell silent and a gloom seemed to settle in on us when we knowed right well one of us had made a big mistake.

"It ain't likely the Union boys knew the general was wounded unless the word trickled through somehow, but it shore appeared like as much. For there was artillery a-firin' on us all that night. Sometimes things got mighty confusin'.

"The next day we heard Stonewall was hit in the left arm in two places and they'd takin' him to a hospital. In about a week we was told the general was dead. Now Lee sent orders for us to keep marchin' even on the day of the funeral. Stonewall woulda wanted it that away.

"I allus said the good Lord took Jackson so the Union could win and free the darkies from their slavery. Yes, Stonewall was a mighty fine general but he was a-standin' between those poor colored folks and their freedom."

We heard the back door open and saw Grandma standing there asking, "What's all this talkin' goin' on out here? You know when Pa gits to tellin' one of those Civil War stories, no one else gits to say one solitary word."

"Shucks in August! I had some hard times myse'f durin' that war and I didn't have no general to hep direct me either.

"I had a mighty tryin' time gittin' the farm work done. Pa's cousin was right he'pful, though. He used to plant the garden. He said not to plant the tomatoes until the oak leaves was as big as sows' ears. He allus planted the winter turnips in August. He was old and stowed up but could shore sing songs all the time he's a-workin'. When he's a-plantin' turnips, he'd sing, `Shirt tail up, shirt tail down, I hope every turnip will weigh ten pound.'

"Pa's other cousin was shot because he warn't goin' to fight against the North. His wife jist begged on bended knee to spare him but they shot him anyway. I'm tellin' ya, the men who wouldn't fight was treated far worse than Northerners. I've seen some mighty hard times in my day."

"We better start home," said Virl. "It will soon be time to do the evening chores. Papa doesn't want us to be late."

"Wait awhile," said Grandma. "You better have some lemonade a-fore you start down that hill. It is hotter than blazes out there."

Grandma gave each of us a big glass of lemonade, so we sat in the shade awhile longer and talked to Grandpa. Since I felt he was the most reliable source of information on matters of religion, I asked him if he had ever been baptized and he said, "Why, yea, way back in North Carolinee. I'se jist a young man when I accepted the Lord and drekly after that I'se baptized in the Yadkin River. Why ye be askin' me that?"

It was then I told him all about the dolls, the teddy bear, and the cats. His eyes began to twinkle and he chuckled to himself, "Now don't you go to worryin', child, you've done no harm. Come here and set by me. I been livin' nigh on to ninety years and I been a-studyin' this good Book from kiver to kiver and I reckon I kin answer yer questions fer ye, if anybody can.

"So yer wonderin' what baptism is. Well, I'll tell ye, it's a way of showin' others what you really believe. Jesus was baptized in the River Jordan by John the Baptist. It ain't likely He'd be doin' somethin' the Good Lord hadn't intended for Him to do."

"Could I be baptized, Grandpa?" asked Virl.

"You sure could, but there's a heap yer goin' ter haf to do first. Yer goin' ter haf to make up yer own mind to accept Jesus as yer own Savior. Yer goin' to have to believe this here old Book. When yer old enough to do that and know what yer about, ye kin be baptized. Nobody gits baptized unless he's a born agin Christian. Now if you'd jist go and git baptized now, it wouldn't mean a sight mor'n putting them there cats in the crik. Nope, ye can't git baptized until ye know what yer doin'."

"Grandpa, I know what I'm doing. I'm old enough to know what I'm doing," I told him.

"Yes, child, but I'm a-hankerin' to find out fer myse'f. You do some readin' for me and then I aim to ask ye a powerful lot o' questions. I don't want no hemmin' and hawin'; I want some answers drekly from yer heart. The first four gospels of the New Testament is what I aim fer you to read fer the beginnin'."

After the reading assignment was made, Grandpa started to talk about himself.

"I'm a-livin' on borried time. A man's allotted three score and ten years to do some sowin' on this old earth, from then on the Good Lord is givin' him time to do some reapin'. These last years have been good t'me. Now with my own little grandchildren here at my old knee a a-skin' fer spirtual lernin', I jist pray I'll be granted sufficient time to make my point clear."

Grandpa called us back from the door as we started to leave, "Come back here a minute. Let's me and you jist bow for a word of prayer." Together we bowed and he made petition to his Lord to grant him wisdom to help us understand the way of salvation and the meaning of baptism.

As we started for home, Virl and Grace ran on ahead, but I walked home a little more thoughtfully than I usually did. I paid little heed to the cow pies in the trail or the salt lick on the hillside. Grandpa had set some ideas astir, ideas too big for me to comprehend, but I planned to fulfill my assignment and to continue to ask questions. Nothing seemed to matter too much, as long as I had Grandpa to answer questions and to pray for me. I felt protected and safe and free.

Chapter Twelve
It Happened One Morning

ଛୀର୍ତ୍ତ

While the green wheat on the sloping hillsides basked in the sunshine and rippled its way to maturity, the timothy and clover that had covered the virgin meadows lay baled and stored in the barn, all 200 tons of a bumper crop waiting to be sold. That part of the summer harvest was finished and the crew of men, including Old Bill, had left in search of other farm work.

Haying time had meant hiring time. Papa believed that to be proficient, a man was needed for each job. He also felt it was his humanitarian responsibility to provide a job for every desarvin' man.

Mama often said, "I really believe your Papa sometimes has more men than he does hay. I keep telling him he puts the cart before the horse."

When Mama would comment on the hired man situation, Grandpa would come to Papa's defense of his employment bureau with quotations from the Bible, such as, "Do unto others as you would have them do unto you," or "What ye do unto the least of these, ye do also unto me."

Regardless of Mama's statements or Grandpa's scriptures, Papa continued to have a big crew of men for the summer haying. Papa also had had a baling crew. Papa's enthusiasm for farming had dimmed a bit the day the barn and the baler burned.

It happened one morning when Papa was making preparations to go to Davenport on business. The barn literally burst into flames in an explosion that sent bales of hay out through the openings.

Papa had rolled the buggy from its shelter and had left it in readiness with fresh axle grease oozing from the hubs. The barn stalls were noisy with the squeaking of harness and the breakfasting of animals.

Flaxie and Lizzie ate their oats while they awaited the neck yoke and another trip to town.

Papa was shaving. He stood before a little fly-specked mirror which hung above the wash bench just in back of the kitchen door. The coal oil lamp in the wall bracket was lit. Its reflector cast a pale yellow glow across Papa's lathered face and made plain the dirty spots on the nearby roller towel. The wash basin on the bench below was steaming with water from the boiling teakettle.

Virl and Grace and I vied for a vantage point to watch Papa draw the straight edge across his foamy beard.

"Stand back and don't bother your Papa while he's shaving," reminded Mama as she went out the back door to get a shirt from the clothesline. Mama ironed the clothes as the need arose. Now Papa needed a shirt to wear to town. The kitchen stove was hot as the teakettle boiled and the flat irons turned sizzling hot.

"It is as hot as a bake oven in here," commented Papa as he added some more hot water to the basin. He dipped the badger hair shaving brush into the water and then into the shaving cup. I watched as the foam flowed over the rim and dripped slowly down the sides, covering the colorful decorations.

Papa dabbed some more of the fluffy mixture over his whiskers, then flicked the razor up and down the strop until the edge could meet the test of splitting a hair. One of my own tresses was offered for the sacrifice. As I handed Papa my sacrificial offering, I remembered Grandpa had said, "The Scriptures say even the hairs of your head are numbered."

As we watched Papa carefully test the razor's edge, we were startled by Mama's screams from the yard.

"The barn's on fire! The barn's on fire! You've got to do something! The barn's on fire!"

Papa, half-shaven, fled in the direction of the blazing barn. Great belches of smoke came from beneath the eaves.

"The barn's on fire!" screamed Mama as she watched the crackling blazes push the smoke skyward. She started running and grabbing frantically at Papa's arm, "Don't go out there. You'll get killed. Oh, God, help us! Somebody do something. The barn's on fire."

Fear gripped me as I watched the giant spectacle of the burning barn. The acrid smell, the crackling sound, and the awesome sight, coupled with Mama's distraught condition and the uncertainty of Papa's safety, sent the tentacles of fear clutching at my very being. There was no fire drill for this sort of thing.

I stood close against the sheltering wall of the house with Grace and Virl close by. We were helpless and afraid to move. Papa was out there somewhere and Mama was crying and praying and wringing her hands. She had often told us she had always been afraid of fire and here it was in all its awful magnitude, leaping out in all directions, ever wider and higher, leaving our family as helpless spectators.

As he ran toward the barn, Papa had gone by and fastened the pasture gate to head off the horses that were running in from the pasture, headed for their stalls and certain destruction. He ran on across the barn lot and into the burning barn. A curtain of smoke whirled down and we all began to cry.

"Oh, my God! Somebody do something," moaned Mama. After what seemed ages, we saw Papa emerging from the barn, desperately trying to get the horses to safety. Suddenly they bolted out into the barnyard, rearing and whinnying. There was a stifling down draft of smoke and cinders. Through our tears we could see the dim figures of Papa and the horses making their way across the barn lot, against a background of roaring flames.

When Papa had the horses safely beyond the barnyard, he leaned helplessly against the orchard fence and watched the walls fall in on a crop of hay. There was a swooshing thud, followed by cinders and sparks, as the freshly refueled fire gathered momentum. The reflected heat became so intense Papa had to move farther away. As he came down the path toward the house, the ashes were falling all around him.

"We gotta get some water on the roof. The house's liable to go, too." Papa's words stirred us into action. A ladder was placed against the wall and a bucket brigade from pump to roof soon splashed the dry, thirsty shingles. We hurried feverishly, spilling water on ourselves and on one another, each of us shouting orders as we tried to empty all of the pails Papa could fill.

Mama carried the pails as Papa filled them at the pump. Virl came up the ladder and Grace and I ran barefooted across the shingles, splashing water as we went. Curious neighbors who had come to look at the burning barn joined our volunteer fire department and relieved Papa at the pump and assisted in dampening the roof of the house.

The fire at the barn was the main attraction, so the house was left to drip as we straggled back through the orchard to look at the last remains of what had so recently stored a bumper hay crop. The fence seemed to serve as a barrier to the danger beyond. We sat upon it, leaned against it, and clung to it for support. It was four boards high with spaces to look through or to serve as toe holds.

Our whole family arranged ourselves along the fence and gazed helplessly at the waning fire. Neighbors continued to come and to go, leaving their sympathies with us. Mama, who was white with shock, and Papa, half-shaven and haggard, seemed to think aloud as they stood watching.

"Whatever started it?"

"Lord only knows. I don't."

"Did anybody get the calf out?"

"I'se blamed lucky to git myse'f out."

"We just can't get along without a barn."

"No, I reckon not."

"What are we going to do?"

"I dunno. I ain't paid the baler crew yet."

"What are we going to do?"

Papa did not answer Mama's question. Out there in that smoldering heap was a cremated hay crop, harnesses, tools, machinery, and the big hay baler. The tangled tentacles of burned steel glowed grotesquely through the flaming embers of what was once our barn.

"We can't do nothin' standin' here. Let's go fix these youngins somethin' to eat."

That evening we ate bread and milk. We were hungry and it tasted good. We sat up late waiting for the fire to die down to a safe degree. We children did not talk much as we stayed close to Mama and Papa for reassurance. I knew they would know what to do no matter what happened to us.

Before going to bed, we went out into the yard to take one last look to see that all danger had passed. We stood huddled together, trying to reconcile ourselves to this disaster. Then Papa's voice cut through the darkness.

"I know I can't afford it, but tomorree I'm goin' to git a loan on the livestock. I simply can't run this ranch without a barn."

It took a year of time, trouble, and money, but Papa did build that new barn. It may not have been a masterpiece, but to us children it was a grand building, offering many delightful hours of recreation. Papa did not replace the baler. Haying was done by a shock-to-mow method which included a hay wagon and a Jackson fork motivated by a derrick system pulled by a team at the back of the barn. Cables carrying a counter balance led from the front gable out across the barnyard, over the orchard fence, and anchored to a sturdy apple tree.

The heavy weight that traveled up and down the cable with each fork load of hay served as a source of fun for Virl and us girls. When the weight hung low over the fence, we grasped the sides of it securely and swung out into space as the derrick team pulled the fork load up the front of the barn. The counterweight went slowly up the cable while we hung precariously below.

When we reached a certain height, we let loose and dropped to the ground. We marked the spot where we landed and a sort of dare base game resulted, with each one of us going a bit higher and dropping a bit further. It was frightening fun.

Papa was behind the barn driving the derrick and assumed we were more gainfully employed in some farm task. The hired man handling the fork ignored our fun. He was a new, hard-featured, cranky fellow who had let us know he considered a family of children an unnecessary evil. As we swung out into space in our hazardous game, he paid little attention to us.

Virl was the winner with the longest drop. My feet were stinging and I was afraid to go any higher. Grace would not give up until she could have one more turn. As she sailed off into space, she called down, "I'm the winner. I can go the highest."

We watched her jerking along in midair, gradually gaining height. Soon we realized she was getting beyond a safe descent.

"Let loose, Grace! Jump!" I called. Then, realizing her danger, I called fearfully, "Hang on, Grace! Hang on! You're too high to jump!"

Virl ran toward the man on the wagon. "Hey, you! Mr. Man, stop the fork!"

"You stupid hyenas. What on earth do you think you're celebrating?" Then he shouted to Papa at the back of the barn. "Hold it! Hold it back there. Now you jack-a-napes run around there, tell your pa to back up that team slow or that kid's agoin' to get her blame neck broken."

"You go, Mollie," said Virl. "I'll stay here and catch her if she falls."

Running to the back of the barn I called, "Back the horses slow, Papa. Grace is hanging on the derrick weight and can't jump down. Back 'em up slow so she won't fall."

Papa looked startled and angry as he started the horses backing. "Whoa. Back. Easy now. You run on," he yelled to me. "Tell Grace to hold on tight. I hope that man's got enough sense not to trip that there fork."

Grace was descending in slow jerks that swung her like a pendulum. "Hold tight, Grace. Hold tight," called Virl, running along beneath her and holding up his arms to catch her if she dropped too soon. Finally she let loose, knocking Virl to the ground with her as she fell. Neither seemed the worse for the experience, but that episode ended our derrick dare game.

Papa came from the back of the barn. The men stopped work to see if Grace was hurt and add their comments to Papa's stern reproof of our dangerous escapade. There were men from the hay mow, and from the second load of hay just arriving from the field. The cross, cranky fellow handling the Jackson fork showed little concern. He bellowed out from atop the load of hay, "Let's get on with this haying. I didn't hire on here to train monkeys for a circus. Keep those brats out of my hair or I'll be shoving off."

Papa winked at one of the other men, commenting, "That wiseacre may not know it, but he jist got hisself fared. I'll put up with a lot, but there ain't nobody goin' to call my youngins brats."

Chapter Thirteen
Catalogue Order from Sears and Roebuck

ഌൟൟ

"That thing fits ye like a saddle on a sow," said Papa, glancing over at Mama as he thumbed through the Sears and Roebuck catalog. "I'm goin' to order ye some house dresses that'll fit ye."

"I kinda like these Mother Hubbards," replied Mama, smoothing out the wrinkles in her slightly ironed dress which hung full and straight, unhampered from the shoulder yoke.

Papa continued to turn the pages of the catalog, putting marks by the articles he intended to order. Twice a year Papa went through this procedure as purchasing agent for the family wardrobe.

It was time for the fall order to be sent. The whole family was seated around the dining room table. Papa turned the wick of the coal oil lamp a little higher and continued to check off his selections. Later he would dictate and I would fill out the order blank.

One time something caused a few days' delay between marking the selections and filling out the order. During that delay Joe went through the catalog and marked his own selections. When Papa started to dictate the order, he found check marks beside everything from wheel chairs to boxing gloves. He was furious. From that time on, the catalog had a reserved spot for safe keeping beside the almanac and the family Bible.

Mama did not have much voice in purchasing for the family, either food or clothing. Papa was the manager of our home in the same manner as he had once managed a store.

"What size dress do ye think you'll need?" asked Papa, getting the measuring tape from the sewing machine drawer. "Or do ye think you'd have time to run up some if I git ye the calico? I see they got it here in red with blue dots, or blue with red dots, or white with blue or red dots. Nice variety. Might git some of each. Then there's a bundle of remnants that's cheaper. It says here, `Save. Remnant bundles. Ten yards of assorted calico, percale, sateen and voile. Lengths from one to four yards. Values to 19¢ a yard. Choice of light or dark colors. Weight two pounds. One bundle 97¢, three for $2.50'. Whatta ye think?"

"Whatever you think. But I can't get much sewing done with all the other work. Maybe I can make these dresses do. Just get things for the children. They all need clothing. Everyone of them needs overshoes this fall," commented Mama, getting up from the table and putting another piece of wood in the heater. Pieces of bark shattered onto the floor as she pushed the large chunk of wood into the flaming belly of the stove. Mama closed the door against the flaming wood using the corner of her apron as a pot holder. She tapped the stove pipe to make it secure in the chimney before she returned to the table where Papa was selecting footwear for the family.

"I'm gittin' the boys these here copper-toed shoes. They oughta keep their toes where they belong. Half-solen' ain't so hard but I can't fix the uppers. Take off yer shoes and let's git yer feet measured."

There was no need to ask for shoes to be removed. When Papa first mentioned copper-toes, there was some under-the-table maneuvering to see who could be first. Shoes were unlaced and ready to be kicked off. Joe, who had found a hard knot in his shoestring, began to cry. Crying was not condoned at catalog time.

"Stop yer whimperin'. Yer liable to have to go barefoot if yer goin' to act like a baby. Now if yer big enough to git hard knots in yer laces, yer big enough to git 'em out."

Papa placed the shoe chart on the floor with Virl as his first customer. "Put yer weight on yer right foot. Don't wrinkle yer toes. This boy's really growin'. Looks like he's goin' to be wearin' a man's size this year. Say, come to think of it, they don't come with copper toes. Both the girls are goin' to git high-top Red Goose shoes again this year."

Papa would go through a session of meticulously measuring our feet, only to order the shoes all in D width and two sizes larger than measured so no one could outgrow his footwear before they were ready for half-soling and a second season of wear.

"Well, I reckon that should have 'em all shod for another year," mused Papa, as he sharpened an indelible pencil with his pearl-handled pocket knife. "You fill out the order," he continued, handing me the pencil and an order blank torn from the back of the catalogue. "You're gittin' better at cipherin' than I am."

"You know," interrupted Mama, "it would be nice to have one of those decorated kerosene lamps to set on that stand in the front room. It would make a better light for seeing to read in there. I've always liked those lamps. They are early American. It would look nice with that braided rug your mother made for us."

"Early American!" retorted Papa. "This is Hawk Creek in the twentieth century. Them big round lamp chimneys is jist to look at. We got to cut corners this year. There jist ain't enough money to go 'round. Put this down," continued Papa, dictating the order, "one bundle remnants, color, dark."

Mama got up from the table. "It's bedtime for you little ones," she said with a sigh. "I guess being in need of money has some good things about it, if a person is just able to see it. Even Shakespeare felt there was when he said, 'Sweet are the uses of adversity, which like a toad, ugly and venomous, wears yet a precious jewel in its head.'"

"Ho-hum! Sometimes I think your mama has more poetry about her than truth. Now this here Shakespeare never had to make out an order to Sears and Roebuck or pay a payment on a loan to build a barn. Who ever heard of a hoppin' toad with jewels in his head? Shakespeare! Poppycock! Let's git this here order finished. You know, I git blamed tared of all that hogwash. Put this down: one pair, four-buckle overshoes. Make that a size bigger than that last pair of shoes."

When the order was finished and sealed in the envelope, a two-cent stamp affixed to the corner, Papa put it up on the sideboard. He put the indelible pencil back in the breast pocket of his bib overalls. "Better git on to bed. We gotta git up early in the mornin'."

I crawled in between the cotton blankets made warm by Grace's sleeping body. I cupped my hand behind the chimney of the nearby lamp and blew out the light. I then tried to repeat from memory, "Sweet are the uses of adversity...."

I awoke the next morning with the sun shining in my eyes and the smell of hotcakes coming from downstairs. I dressed quickly, called Grace, and went across the hall to waken

Virl and Joe. Virl pretended to be sound asleep until I approached the bed. Suddenly a pillow landed against my face. I threw it back, only to have a second pillow hit me broadside.

Hearing the familiar sounds of a pillow fight, Grace came from across the hall armed with more fine-feathered ammunition. Each of us stood as an open target as we exchanged pillow for pillow.

Flour sack cases were soon pulled off. The striped ticking slammed against heads, bowed to take the blows of pillows in full flight. Feathers began to slip from dog-eared corners. Dust and down filled the air.

Grace and I returned pillow for pillow as the boys bobbled about the bed like big grasshoppers. Joe and Virl tried to claim the largest pillow, each grabbing it at the same instant. A tug of war followed until the pillow came apart at the seams, releasing a cloud of feathers that were suddenly everywhere.

"What's goin' on up there?" called Papa from the foot of the stairway. That voice of authority brought an immediate cease fire. Everything went quiet like the lull following a storm.

"You all better hit the floor. 'Cause if I come up there, you'll wish I hadn't."

It was not long until the four of us were downstairs, washed and ready for breakfast. Mama set a pile of hotcakes next to the syrup pitcher. "Go in the bedroom," she said, looking at me. "And get John off the pottychair. Put those brown rompers on him and get him in here for his breakfast."

The potty-chair was a work of Papa's handicraft. It consisted of an apple box set on end with the top removed and placed like a shelf in the center. A comfortable circle was cut in the shelf and a cup-like potty placed beneath. It was from this seat of training I rescued John each morning.

As I entered the bedroom, I found the seat deserted. John had become tired of the apple box treatment and had gone outside. I found him in front of the house, running, stark naked, up and down the wooden sidewalk. I chased him and caught him and spanked him on his bare behind.

"Let that child alone!" called Mama, tapping the window with the hotcake turner. "If there's any spanking to be done around here, your Papa and I will do it. Go put some clothes on that child like I told you to do."

John's pink bottom was soon concealed beneath a heavy outing flannel diaper applied in a triangular wad and anchored with a big brass safety pin. There were no underpants available, so the diaper was worn for decency's sake as his rompers were becoming much too short to fasten together between his legs. The old brown rompers hung like a scalloped skirt, flapping loosely at the sides.

"That child will get bow-legged if we don't get him some underthings to wear," commented Mama as she watched John waddle into the kitchen, straddling the cumbersome diaper. "I wish your papa hadn't sealed that mail order," said Mama as she poured some more pancake batter on the big black griddle.

Finally the family was gathered around the kitchen table, each in his usual place. Mama insisted it was mannerly, as well as important, to sit together and eat as a family each mealtime.

More pancakes were stacked on the platter and Papa's cup was filled with steaming coffee from the big enameled coffee pot. I noticed Papa looked tired as he asked for the butter to be passed. He buttered his pancakes, then put butter and syrup on John's pancake since he was sitting next to him in the high chair. Papa cut John's pancake into little pieces before he started eating his own breakfast, and as he ate he began to talk between bites.

"As I said before, we are goin' to haf to cut corners. I wish there was some other way, but since we lost the barn and the baler I've done my best. I've built a new barn, bought machinery, cut fence posts and farwood to get some cash, but seems like folks ain't got money to even buy hay like they used to. I need another cup of coffee."

"I realize times aren't like they used to be," commented Mama as she filled the pitcher with some more homemade Mapeline syrup. "I was reading that some folks say we are having a financial depression."

"Well," retorted Papa, "call it what you want! I've sed before, hard times has hit. We've finally come to the point when we are goin' to hef to do what they do over the river."

"And what do they do over the river?" asked Virl, who had to have an answer to everything.

"They do without! Eat yer breakfast and stop asking questions that even the good Lord can't answer."

After a few minutes when all was quiet around the breakfast table, Papa continued, "Well, Virl, when you finish eatin', run that catalog order up to the mailbox and be sure to put the flag up. Guess I did somethin' worthwhile when I talked those fellows into gettin' Rural Free Delivery for the Hawk Creek Canyon mail. You know, I think if we work at tryin' to keep our heads above water, times are goin' to hef to get better."

I could not finish my breakfast because Papa looked so tired, but those feathers scattered all over the upstairs bedroom worried me more than anything else. What if Papa found out?

Chapter Fourteen
The Glint and Glow Pictures

ဆာလ

"**I**'d like to have ye meet the missus," was the extent of Papa's introduction as he ushered the stranger into the kitchen just at supper time. "Don't believe I got the name, but this here's the family. Reckon we can put ye up for the night. Jest hang yer coat over on one of those hooks in the corner and make yerse'f to home."

"Ho do, ma'am. Hope I won't put you out none," mumbled the stranger, looking over the kitchen full of children.

"How do you do," answered Mama, adding some more milk to the gravy and stirring it until it spilled over the edges of the big black frying pan.

We children were not introduced. We stood awkwardly about the kitchen watching Papa make the stranger feel right at home. Papa put some warm water from the teakettle into the wash pan and dippered some cold water from the pail to mix with it so the stranger might wash his hands and face. This red carpet treatment was of special interest to us because we had to wash in cold water.

The stranger was fairly well dressed and his clothes were neat and clean. I noticed he had put a satchel and a briefcase on the floor beneath his coat. He looked more important than most of the people who had stopped at our house for the night. When he had finished washing he made an unsuccessful attempt to find a clean dry spot on the roller towel.

Mama handed him a clean towel from the pile of clothes on a nearby chair. He dried his face on the wrinkled towel and then reached up and put it on the roller, tossing the dirty towel over to me. I blushed with the thought the strange man had even noticed me. Quickly I walked out to the porch and put the soiled towel in the dirty clothes barrel.

"Run down to the cellar and get a jar of peaches," Mama called after me. "Better bring some of those pickled beets, too."

After supper, Mama and I put clean sheets on the bed in the boy's bedroom. They had to vacate to make room for Papa's house guest. Whenever Old Bill was away we used his room for overnight visitors. This time Old Bill, with a flaming case of gout, was at home enjoying his misery. Only a very unwelcome guest would be sent to the bunk house, so to provide a spare bed, it took some behind-the-scenes maneuvering, with five of us children and a permanent hired man. Virl was happy to sleep on the sofa, but Grace and I were quite indignant to have Joe and John spend the night at the foot of our bed.

The stranger ate a second helping of hotcakes for breakfast. He was a friendly man and Papa enjoyed talking to him.

"If ye ever happen back through these parts, stop in and visit with us."

"I just might do that. I really appreciate the hospitality. Before I leave, though, I'd like to tell you and your missus about a real opportunity for you folks to get some pictures of this handsome family of yours. Don't know which one of you they get all their good looks from, but you have some mighty fine-looking children."

"Well, I sorta agree with ye. My oldest girl here," boasted Papa, patting me on the head, "got the blue ribbon at the fair for bein' the prettiest baby girl in Lincoln County. Never got around to enterin' the rest of 'em, but you can bet your bottom dollar they'da all walked off with the first prize if they'da had a chance."

"You ought to have some pictures taken of these children," suggested the stranger.

"She had her picture taken that day at the fair. Run in the bedroom and git it out of the trunk and show it to the man."

The stranger took the picture from me and looked at it carefully. "This would make a wonderful enlargement."

Reaching into the inside pocket of his coat, he brought out a pack of thin envelopes secured with a rubber band.

"There's a lucky envelope in this stack," smiled the stranger, snapping the band and cautiously working up to his surprise. "It contains a coupon for a free enlargement for the picture of your choice. You may draw anyone of these envelopes. Let's see how lucky you are, sir. A free enlargement of this prize-winning picture may be yours for the asking."

"Don't know's I'm askin'," came Papa's curt reply as he recognized this gimmick as a bit of salesmanship. This apparent thought had an alienating effect on Papa's cordiality. "Guess you're barkin' up the wrong tree. Don't reckon I'd want one a them enlargements, anyway, when I got some real life-sized ones runnin' around here every day."

While Papa was talking, the stranger kept tapping his briefcase, the contents of which had remained a mystery. It was a dark leather case fastened with a shiny lock. Quickly he opened it and spread his display of pictures about the room, propping them up on the kitchen chairs. It was my first art exhibit.

There was one of an old lady with a double chin standing by her goateed husband who was uncomfortably posed with hat in hand and gaiters showing. There was a brown-eyed baby boy in a long christening dress and a lovely girl in a bridal gown. There were pictures on every chair and more left in the briefcase. Each enlargement was vividly tinted until eyes sparkled and cheeks glowed.

Papa was favorably impressed with this grand display. "You got some mighty fine-lookin' pictures there. That one of the soldier boy looks like he's a-goin' to speak."

"These are just a few of the lucky people who drew the coupon for the free enlargements. Absolutely free! Why don't you take a chance? That's what Columbus did, you know. Not every man has a good-looking family like yours."

"Well, I want you to know thet I ain't a pushover fer one of these here silver-tongued salesmen, but since ye say I might git one free-gratis, hand over them envelopes."

Papa drew one of the envelopes from the center of the pack. The stranger took it from Papa and tore it open, removing a slip of paper with the words "Coupon for Two Enlargements."

The stranger became very excited and showed he was unduly impressed with Papa's lucky draw. "This is the very first time that anyone, to my knowledge, has ever drawn this envelope with two free enlargements. How lucky can you get? This baby picture is fine for one of the enlargements," he said as he tucked it into his briefcase. "What other picture shall I send in for you?"

Mama became concerned at this turn of events. "I don't like to take a chance of having our pictures lost. We don't have any extra copies."

"Don't you worry, ma'am, here's my card. Remember, I represent the Glint and Glow Picture Company of New York and I'll personally be responsible for your pictures. What other one would you like to send along with this blue ribbon baby picture?"

After a family consultation around the box of treasured pictures, Mama and Papa decided they would send a picture of Papa that had been taken before they were married.

"Now I see where the children get their good looks," commented the stranger as he put Papa's picture in the case with mine. While we had been sorting pictures, the salesman had repacked his samples and stood ready to depart. The second picture was all he was waiting for.

"If everybody was as lucky as you are, my company would go broke," was the stranger's parting remarks. "Goodbye. See you in about six weeks."

Papa was mending a harness in the tool shed the day the pictures were delivered. It had been two months since the lucky drawing. Mama's apprehensions concerning the safety of my baby picture had been mounting with each passing week.

When the salesman came to the house, Mama sent me to the tool shed to get Papa. I ran all the way out through the orchard and across the barnyard.

"Papa," I called, "our pictures are here. A different man brought them. Mama wants you to come to the house."

Papa hung the harness on a hook and wiped his oily hands on a gunny sack before leaving the shed.

"He's a different salesman, Papa. He's a big, fat man."

By the time Papa and I had arrived at the house, the salesman had the pictures unwrapped and standing against the wall.

"Well, sir, how do you like the pictures?" questioned the stranger, disregarding an introduction. He shook Papa's hand enthusiastically and beamed patronizingly at all of us.

"How do, sir. Guess I really was lucky, wasn't I? Much obliged fer deliverin' fer me. I'se figurin' to hef to pick 'em up at the depot one of these days. Whatever happened to yer sidekick who come through here awhile back, handin' out these free enlargements?"

"Oh, he's been assigned to another part of the country. I make the deliveries and do the collecting. My job is to deliver the pictures and present the bill."

"Bill? There ain't goin' to be no bill. I drew the envelope with the two free enlargements."

"You are exactly right. Your enlargements are entirely free. My company was sure you'd want these lovely pictures protected and displayed under unbreakable glass and with solid frames. Master craftsmen have done the job for you," continued the salesman, as he slipped a wooden mallet from his coat pocket and pounded on the face of the picture. "They used the best unbreakable glass and fine polished hardwood. You get all this for a nominal fee of seven dollars per picture. Only fourteen dollars and your cherished pictures are protected for a lifetime."

Papa was angry. His blue eyes flashed like the sparkling of the tinted picture.

"Why, that old shyster!"

"Well, sir. I only make the deliveries and do the collecting. I didn't take the order."

"Now, you listen here. I didn't give no order and you ain't goin' to do no collectin'."

This heated discussion continued for some time. There was finally an offer by the salesman to remove the pictures from the frames and to reduce the fee to cover only the cost of the original framing. Papa was visibly shaken, so we children kept our distance. Mama tried to keep out of the argument but she did offer one suggestion.

"Those pictures wouldn't be much good to us without the frames."

"Guess not," conceded Papa. "Ain't much else we can do now but keep 'em, I reckon. But I'm here to tell ye one thing—someone ought to put the law on that two-timin' swindler. Goin' around offerin' free pictures and then chargin' a man fer 'em. That old blatherskite needs to be prosecuted to within an inch of his life."

"Well, sir, I only make the deliveries and do the collecting. You are getting more than your money's worth with solid hardwood frames and unbreakable glass."

When the fee was finally collected, the salesman left abruptly and, without further comment, Papa went over to the stove and poured a cup of black coffee from the pot on the back of the range. He sat down by the table to drink the coffee and to let his anger cool.

Mama and we children admired the pictures. We tried to decide just where they should be hung. Joe and John crowded closer to get a better view. Soon they started pushing and over went Papa's picture, face down on the floor with a resounding crash. At the sound of breaking glass, Papa tipped over his coffee as he jumped from his chair.

"Watch your language in front of the children," warned Mama, as Papa's anger flared to new heights.

Joe and John both got a spanking before Papa returned to the tool shed. I swept the unbreakable glass into the dustpan, and Mama put the pictures out of sight in the back of the bedroom closet.

The next Saturday, our family went over to our neighbors to help with the butchering. After the usual neighborly greetings, we were invited into the living room by Mr. Stickleburger.

"Come right on into the parlor. I want you to see the pictures I got of me and my old lady."

"Now, how did you happen to get 'em?" inquired Papa, giving Mama a knowing wink, as he surveyed the brightly tinted enlargements on the living room wall.

"Well, to tell you the truth, I'se mighty lucky. A fellar came by here awhile back and give me a chance to get some pictures, and I'll be blamed if I didn't draw the envelope with the two free enlargements. How do you like 'em?"

"Well," says Papa, critically eyeing the pictures, "they're real nice and life-like, but them frames look mighty expensive. Ain't they made of solid polished hardwood?"

"Yep, and that there is unbreakable glass."

Chapter Fifteen
A School Day in October

ഇൽ

"Well, the frost is on the punkin," said Papa. "Better wear your jackets this mornin'. Old Jack Frost is calling a mite early, don't you think?"

"It'll warm up," said Mama. "We haven't had Indian summer yet. Look at that blue sky. October is my favorite month. It reminds me of the poem, 'October's Bright Blue Weather':

> O sun and skies and clouds of June,
> And flowers of June together,
> Ye cannot rival for one hour
> October's bright blue weather!

"Children, you better run on to school. You'll be late if you don't hurry."

It was Virl's turn to carry the big family lunch pail, which I had filled with hard-boiled eggs and peanut butter and apple jelly sandwiches. The gallon pail was an old lard container with the Banner Meat Company pig visible from the side.

Grace and Virl left for school while I was helping Joe lace his new copper-toed shoes. Joe was just six years old and found that getting ready for school was sometimes a problem, especially after a summer of going barefooted every day.

John came into the kitchen wearing a coat and wanting to accompany us to school. Joe put his arm around John and said, "Don't cry, little bud. When you are six years old you can go to school with Mamie, Didi, and Burr." Joe always had a nickname for everyone in the family and soon Mama and Papa were calling us Mamie, Didi, and Burr.

As I started to school, I heard Mama say, "Come with me, John. I'll read you a story of Peter Rabbit and Mr. MacGregor."

Joe and I hurried through the orchard and on to the dusty road leading up the canyon to school. No matter how hard we tried to be early, every school morning we worried about being late. Papa always knew if we had been late because the teacher put the number of days tardy on our report cards. Papa said being on time was more important than having your shoes shined.

I was proud of the Hawk Creek Canyon road, which was Papa's work of art, maintained in neat and smooth condition. He was the road boss and hired men to help run the road equipment, which was kept at our place.

As we hurried along Papa's Highway, as we called it, there were many interesting things that would distract us. There were fresh porcupine tracks across the dust near the old deserted pear orchard. Overhead a flock of Canadian geese were flying south in perfect formation, honking as they flew.

As I rounded the last curve, there was Virl and Grace watching the geese. Virl asked, "Where do you think that old gander is leading the flock? I'd sure like to know what the country looks like outside of Hawk Creek Canyon."

The new white schoolhouse was visible about a quarter of a mile up the road, partially hidden in a stand of pine trees on a knoll above the roadway. Next door was the old school building now serving as a woodshed. It was an unpainted structure with missing windows and doors. Mama often talked about the days she had spent in that old building, teaching the Hawk Creek school before she was married to Papa.

"I taught all eight grades and at that time there were a great many students; now there are only a few. I don't understand why so many families are leaving the canyon farms."

As I was pondering on the things Mama had often told me about the old school, I heard the warning bell ring and I knew we had fifteen minutes to reach the classroom.

The four of us dashed into the front hall just as the teacher was ringing the tardy bell. The bell was hung in the tower on the roof and tolled by a rope hanging through the ceiling in the hallway.

"Good morning," greeted Miss Coleman, waiting to usher us into the classroom as soon as we had hung our jackets on the coat rack. Each student had a personal hook above which his name was posted. Also, names were above the tin cups hanging by the water pail under a shelf where the lunch pails were placed.

There were ten pupils enrolled in school so only part of the desks were used and the rest were pushed back against the walls. Each person was assigned a desk and mine was at the back of the room, under the big wall clock that chimed every hour. Right at nine o'clock, Miss Coleman had what she called "opening exercises."

After the flag salute, she went to the organ to accompany us while we sang the "Good Morning" song. "I want everyone of you singing. Let's have a smile on every face. Ready—sing:

Good morning to you, good morning to you.
We're all in our places
With sunshiny faces.
Good morning to you, good morning to you.
For this is the way
To start a new day.
Good morning to you, good morning to you.

Please take your seats and start studying your reading lessons."

The somber faces of George Washington and Abraham Lincoln looked down from their pictures, which hung behind the teacher's desk. The austere looks made me think that preparation of assignments was serious business. I wished we had some pretty pictures to brighten the room. Besides the presidents' pictures, the only things I could see were dark green chalkboards, pull-down maps, a faded globe, and a bookcase full of outdated encyclopedias. Thumbtacks held alphabet cards above the chalkboards and a phonics chart on the wall by the air-tight heater.

During the first part of the morning session, each grade was called to come to the recitation bench for reading and arithmetic classes. Since I was the only seventh grader, I had silent reading at my desk and some of the time took Joe to the phonics chart to drill him on sounds.

There was a brief recess during the forenoon. During this break, we had drinks of water and went to the outdoor toilets, which were situated several yards from the schoolhouse. These two outhouses were on opposite sides of the playground under some large pine trees that housed squirrels and chipmunks. On a small shelf was last year's catalogue ready for its intended purpose.

Recess over, we returned to the classroom. Spelling tests were written on the blackboard as Miss Coleman dictated the lists. Any misspelled words had to be written on paper twenty times each and if misspelled a second time, they were to be written fifty times each.

When we told Papa the way our teacher taught spelling, he said that what we needed was the Blue Back Speller like he used in North Carolina. He had had to learn to spell words both forward and backward. He gave us an example by spelling balloon. "Now when I spelled balloon, I spelled it like this: BA, double-L double-O, N; then N, double-O double-L, AB."

When I told Miss Coleman I wanted to spell like Papa did, she said she had never heard of anything so ridiculous.

I had just finished my history lesson when the clock struck twelve. Every pupil was ready for lunch. Miss Coleman said, "You are excused for lunch time. Turn, stand, pass."

During the nice weather in the fall, we climbed to the slanting roof of the barn and ate our lunches in the sunshine. The school barn was built close to the hillside and the roof was covered with pine needles. Students sat in groups, sharing food from the family lunch pails. Sometimes we traded food. I practically drooled as I watched the bright red Jell-o sparkling in the sunshine as Betty placed a spoon in it.

"I'll trade you a hard-boiled egg for your Jell-o, if you'd like," I urgently suggested. We traded and I was her friend for the rest of the school year.

We never had Jell-o at our house since Papa would not allow it to be included on our grocery list. Papa classified it as hot air and rabbit tracks. I pledged Grace and Virl to secrecy, never to tell Papa I had traded my egg for a cup of Jell-o.

As we continued eating our lunches, we cracked the hard-boiled eggs on our heads and carefully removed the shells. Blue jays scolded at us from the nearby trees and chipmunks scampered about, gathering pine nuts for their winter cache.

After lunches were finished and lids were put back on the lunch pails, we made necklaces from pine needles and looked for nuts in the mature pine cones.

"I can tell your fortune," boasted Betty, placing a pine needle chain around my neck. "I can tell what kind of a man you are going to marry some day."

Betty, the oldest girl in the school, became the center attraction with this startling announcement. We wondered what magical powers she could display. Mysteriously she began, button by button, to reveal my fortune.

"Rich man, poor man, beggar man, thief,

Doctor, lawyer, merchant, chief."

As Betty continued this chant, she searched for buttons to determine my future. When she ended with beggar man, I was disappointed.

Virl came to my rescue by exclaiming, "That's a lot of tomfoolery. Don't believe a word she says."

Sounds of rattling halter chains and munching of oats in the horses' feed boxes came from the barn below as we left the roof for the playground. The Davidson children took turns feeding the horse oats and hay from the back of the buggy. We tried to coax Papa to let us drive Old Lizzie and the buggy to school, but he would always reply, "Shank's mare got me to school. Guess you ain't too good to travel the same way."

Miss Coleman came out of the school building and walked quickly across the playground. Her full, pleated skirt rippled about her slender figure. She was young and very enthusiastic about her first teaching job. During the first week of school, she had added crepe paper window curtains. Papa, clerk of the school board, had voiced his disapproval.

"The winders of a schoolhouse was made to let in the light and not to be fancied up with a lot of petticoat ruffles."

We were soon following directions as Miss Coleman directed us to form a circle and join hands so we could play Drop the Handkerchief.

"Drop your hands and stand where you are. Grace, you are 'it'. Take this handkerchief and run around the outside of the circle. Drop it behind someone who will pick it up and chase you around the circle. See if you can get to the vacant spot before you are touched with the handkerchief.

"Run around the outside, Grace, and drop the handkerchief. The rest of us will sing a song while Grace is running. Everybody sing with me now:

Itisket, Itasket, a green and yellow basket,
I wrote a letter to my love and on the way I dropped it,
I dropped it, I dropped it!"

Grace dropped the handkerchief behind Virl. I could see by the expression on his face he considered this a very sissy game and was not about to participate. The men teachers we had had the last three years had let us play such rough-and-ready games as King of the Mountain and Tin Can Soccer. Papa had tried to hire men teachers but this year no man had applied for the job. Papa's opinion was "A man can make those youngin's toe the line as well as learnin' them to cipher." Mama said a woman teacher would teach some poetry and literature and give them some special things to think about.

Miss Coleman said it was time to go into the school room before we had finished the game. She gave us some chores to do before we did our lessons. The girls were to clean the backboards and chalk trays while the boys got some fresh water for the pail by the drinking cups. Then we each were told to take erasers and clean them by pounding them on the pine trees near the schoolhouse. Miss Coleman put new chalk in all the chalk trays.

At one o'clock, the lower grades were to start art lessons and to learn to color with crayons and stay within the lines, while the upper grades had silent reading. The Traveling Library box had been delivered to the school, so each of us were to select a book. Virl chose The Fire Fiend, a book that described the prevention of forest fires. Betty took a book about the Alaska Eskimos, and I chose one called The Goops, with instructions about good manners. I planned to take the book home and teach my family some good manners Mama had been talking about.

I memorized a poem called "The Disgusting Goops":

The Goops they lick their fingers,
The Goops they lick their knives,
They spill their broth
On the table cloth,
They lead disgusting lives.

I planned that everyone at our house was going to have good manners and not be a family of Goops.

After a short recess, Miss Coleman decided to spend the rest of the day practicing for the Halloween program. We were going to have a play about Rip Van Winkle. Virl was to be Rip Van Winkle and I was Dame Van Winkle. Grace was our daughter and Joe was a Little Keg Man of the Mountain. Other pupils were taking the part of Nicholas Vedder, Brom Dutcher, and Van Bummel.

We put up a large curtain across the end of the room to make a stage for an evening program. All the community had been invited to attend. We had only one more week to bring cornstalks and pumpkins to decorate the room.

Miss Coleman's eyes sparkled with enthusiasm as she turned the pages of Washington Irving's book with her well-manicured fingernails and told us stories of the Katskill Mountain country. I thought it was so good to have a lady teacher who had us do exciting things. I was glad there had been no male applicants for the Hawk Creek school that fall. It seemed to me the men teachers we had had were either novices or old masters getting in one more year before calling it quits. I had heard Papa say, "We need a man for the school jobs. Splitting far wood and doing janitor work is just good exercise for one of those fancy fellers who do nothing but push a pencil all day. Yep, I'll har a man any day 'for I'll sign up one of those city gals and then have to wait on her hand and foot."

"Very well, it's time to dismiss for the day. Put away all your costumes," ordered Miss Coleman. "And Virl, I want you to sprinkle some of that red sweeping compound on the floor before you start home."

I knew Virl was having extra jobs to do because he refused to play Drop the Handkerchief. I felt sorry for him and decided I would help so we could go home together.

The walk home was quite time-consuming any season of the year, but especially so during the fall. Roadside attractions were many and rest stops were frequent. Sounds of pine cones could be heard dropping from the pine trees as squirrels jumped from limb to limb. My responsibilities of being the oldest child were soon forgotten. The sides of the road were sheltered with bushes of ripe elderberries that invited sampling. Rows of pine trees stood like sentinels, interspersed with aspens that applauded me with their quacking leaves as my world of fantasy ran the gamut of imagination.

I was jolted back to reality when I thought of Papa's attitude about the Halloween program. He must never know something I had done last August had caused the school board to hire Miss Coleman.

Before the school board had made their choice, I had secretly looked over the applications Papa had in the top sideboard drawer. Virl and Grace had been with me. It happened one day when Mama was reading and Papa was at a neighbor's. We took the letters, pictures and all, out to the far side of the orchard.

There were eight letters. After reading the applications aloud to Grace and Virl, I spread them out on the ground. We called a board meeting to order to select our future teacher. Each letter had a photograph paper clipped to the top. We took each picture off and passed it around for approval or disapproval.

Our school board meeting was interrupted by Papa's return from the neighbor's. Quickly we clipped the pictures to the letters and returned them to the envelopes. Virl and Grace, sworn to secrecy, went to meet Papa while I ran to the house to return the letters to the sideboard drawer.

When Miss Coleman arrived to teach our school, the school directors, which consisted of Papa and two of our neighbor men, could not figure out how they had become confused about the picture of the teacher they had hired by mail. They had chosen a plain-looking country girl whom they thought would be happy in the Hawk Creek school.

Papa found himself confronted with such accusations as, "I wonder whose idea it was to hire that cute little trick," or "It looks like we better be checkin' up on these old directors. This school business is a might serious thing."

At supper time that night when Papa was complaining about a silly Halloween program, Mama interrupted and voiced her opinion. "I think it is important that the children learn about Rip Van Winkle. It is a Washington Irving classic."

Chapter Sixteen
The Halloween Program

✥

*I*t was the night of the Halloween program. There was a bustle throughout our house as our whole family attempted to get ready at the same time. Joe had lost one of his shoes. Grace's petticoat was too long for her dress. Papa was trimming Virl's hair, and Mama was dressing John in his best rompers.

As Mama went about the room, she continued talking whether anyone was listening or not. She was explaining the literary accomplishments of Washington Irving.

"Washington Irving was the youngest of eleven children. He used to write under the pen name of Jonathan Oldstyle. A pen name is a name used by an author instead of his own name. It is often called a pseudonym or a nom de plume.

"It was about a hundred years ago that Irving wrote about Rip Van Winkle. It was included in his Sketch Book, along with the "Legend of Sleepy Hollow." I hope you children know your parts for the play tonight. You are lucky to have a teacher who is interested in things like this."

"Lucky!" grunted Papa. "You know, I have a hard enough time to git these youngin's up in the mornin' without this young whippersnapper of a schoolmarm teachin' 'em how to sleep for a hundred years."

"Not a hundred," interrupted Virl. "I only sleep for twenty years."

"Well, I ain't a-carin' how long you sleep," said Papa, accidentally snipping the edge of Virl's ear.

"Ouch! What you trying to do? Cut my ears off?"

"Don't go snifflin' now. If you'd hold still your ears wouldn't git in the way. Might be a good idea if the whole lot of you had your ears notched. A person could tell which one was which, 'specially when you git rigged out in all that get-up.

"This whole affair is jist a pack of foolishment. It is gittin' so a teacher's contract jist don't mean nothin' anymore. Now go on outside and bresh the hair offin' you."

I wondered why it was Papa talked like this. I believed that under his rash statements he was really in favor of it all. Papa liked being with people and people liked Papa. He liked rhymes and songs and games. Perhaps he was on the defensive because of the contrast of his limited education and Mama's encyclopedic mind.

I was proud of Mama. I realized her knowledge of many things far exceeded that of any teacher we had ever had. I was glad she spoke out in defense of Miss Coleman and the Halloween program.

As I stood there ironing Papa's white shirt, I kept repeating the lines of Dame Van Winkle for the part I was to play later that evening.

"Yes, hunting. Hunting! Fishing! Fishing, the whole day long and your family going around here half-starved and naked. Look at these children. When do you expect to get them anything to wear?"

"Well," answered Virl, coming in the back door, "I was helping Dame Vedder get her corn in yesterday."

"Yes, that's just it," I continued in my best Dame Van Winkle voice, as high and rusty as I could make it. "Always helping someone else but never tending to your own business. And if you haven't got your finger in somebody else's business, you're down at the inn, spinning yarns. It's just about time you were tending to your own work."

I pretended to kick at the dog and grab at one of my children as I continued to nag. "Come here and get to work! Let me catch a one of you following in the tracks of your good-for-nothing father."

Papa brought my rehearsal to an end by asking for his shirt. "Come on now. Finish that shirt. We gotta be up at that blame schoolhouse in less than an hour. Do you know what time it's a gittin' to be? Git a move on, you."

When Papa gave the commands, the family went into high gear. It wasn't long until we were all getting into the wagon, our conveyance for traveling when all of us went any place. There was a high spring seat in front for Mama and Papa and straw on the floor of the wagon bed for a couple old quilts and us children.

We put the box of sandwiches and the big pan full of cake under the wagon seat so no one would sit on it by mistake. The food was for the refreshments that followed the program. While I was helping make the sandwiches, Mama had commented, "This bread didn't raise. I'm going to have to get a new starter. That old starter is going sour. That applesauce cake is good enough without any frosting. I'm going to take it just the way it is.

"I'm going to put my cake out for people to eat. I'm not going to be like Bessie Stickleburger. Every time she takes a cake anywhere, she puts it in some corner and then when everyone is through eating, she accidentally finds it and announces she is going to have cake for her children's lunches next week. Here, wrap these up in some dish towels and don't let me forget them when we are ready to leave."

I had not forgotten the food. I had eaten very little supper and was hungry before we ever got started on our way.

"Git that dog out of the wagon," said Papa as he climbed up on the seat. "He will tip that lantern over if you ain't kerful."

"The children are taking the dog along with them tonight," commented Mama. "Rover is going to be in the play. He is going to be Wolf, Rip Van Winkle's dog."

"So now we got the school going to the dogs. What will she be asking for next! One of the horses?"

It was quite dark by the time we reached the schoolhouse. It had not taken very long because the horses had trotted most of the way. We had all been rather quiet during the trip, for it was an important occasion to have our whole family dressed up and going some place together.

There was a light in the schoolhouse when we arrived. Papa drove the wagon right up to the front door and we unloaded lunch, dog, and all. There were two men across the school yard unhitching their horses and preparing to tie them to the backs of the wagons.

The horses were suddenly startled by the sound of an approaching car. Headlights beamed up the hill ahead of Uncle and his new Model T. Papa pulled back on the lines and set the brake on the wagon. The other men grasped the halters and tried to steady their teams. There was confusion and shouting everywhere.

"Keep that blame jitney off'n these school grounds! Whata you wanta cause? A runaway?"

"Whoa, now. Easy, girls! There oughta be a law to keep those snortin' go-devils off'n the road. It jist ain't safe no more for man nor beast."

"I'm here to tell ye that feller ain't got no sense driven that flivver right up amongst these here horses."

Uncle parked the Ford right in the light of the windows. He was soon surrounded by young people who had come for the program. He demonstrated the movable parts and tried out the horn several times, much to the consternation of the horse wranglers.

"Git off'n the runnin' boards so the missus and I can git out. Don't none of you youngin's bother this car and I'll take all of ye for a ride one of these days. Man, this shore is the way to travel. Don't have to buy no hay for this old nag."

"You might not have to buy any hay," retorted one of the men. "But you shore as-as—reckon I gotta mind my language on the school grounds—but you shore a-goin' to find yourself a-payin' for some mighty valuable horse flesh if you ain't keerful."

"That's a-tellin' him, Seth," remarked another teamster. "Mark my words, that gadget maker of a Henry T. Ford is goin' to be the ruination of this country yet."

The school bell started ringing, which was the teacher's signal for all of us to come in and get ready for the program to start. As we went in through the hallway, the men stopped to comment about the shiny tin cups which were hanging in a labeled row along the wall.

"Well, what do you know! Modern plumbing. My youngsters better not git so highfalutin' they can't drink outer their old man's dipper."

The parents and visitors were soon seated. Coats and jackets were piled high across the teacher's desk. In one corner of the room two women were trying to get the coal oil stove started to heat water for the coffee. Millers were flying about the gasoline light as one of the men pumped some more air into the lantern.

I stood back of the curtain and peeked out at the audience until Miss Coleman saw me. She reminded me that we were to sit quietly on the recitation bench until she was ready to start the program.

Virl brought Rover backstage and tied him to a chair. Miss Coleman stepped through the curtains and we could hear her welcoming the people to the Hawk Creek School program. Families from miles around had come to spend the evening. The audience was quiet except for one baby who would not stop crying.

The first number was a flag drill. We stomped about the stage, each carrying a little flag and trying to keep time to a march played by Miss Coleman on the organ. Following the singing of "America," we lined up across the stage to spell Halloween with a letter for each child. Someone in the audience was pointing at me and I noticed I had the "W" upside down.

Following the card tricks, we girls, dressed in crepe paper costumes, performed the dance of the autumn leaves. We were golden, brown, and yellow. We dipped and swirled and floated about the stage in a meaningless routine. The organ groaned out a plaintive melody that spoke of the sadness of falling leaves.

Every time the curtain closed, the audience applauded enthusiastically. We were not sure if they were glad the number was finished or whether they honestly enjoyed it all.

Everyone of us had a recitation to give. These were arranged intermittently throughout the program. Sometimes two children stood in front of the curtain and shared a recitation.

Grace and another girl each held a jack-o-lantern and repeated these verses. One would ask:

"Can you tell me what it means
When the winds go wailing by,
 And witches with their black cats
On brooms go riding high?
When grotesque, grinning faces
About the windows peer,
And ghosts with hollow voices
From spooky shades appear?"
Then the other one would answer:
"It means that Miss October,
Before she slips away,
Gives us, to remember her,
A jolly holiday;
She brings spooks, fays and fairies
From many an ancient scene;
It means that all the country
Is keeping Halloween."

While they were speaking, I stood right in back of the curtain ready to prompt if either one forgot a line. During the days of practice, I had learned all the parts of the program by heart.

The highlight of the program, the play "Rip Van Winkle," was a huge success. The audience laughed and clapped from the first scene when Dame Van Winkle tells Old Rip he is a good-for-nothing hound until the end when he comes back to his native village after a twenty-year sleep.

The first scene took place in Rip's home. Rover played the part of Wolf and lay at his master's feet, ignoring the audience and enjoying his first time on the stage. Rip was cleaning his gun, surrounded by all the children in the school. I, as Dame Van Winkle, stood over the washboard, rubbing and nagging. Beneath a clothesline stretched across the stage stood an ironing board with a shirt on one end and a flat iron on the other. Rip's chair was the only other stage property.

Since this was my main scene in the play, I overdid my acting and made Dame Van Winkle, the character Washington Irving portrayed, as one who later was to die in a fit of passion at a New England peddler. Virl was a true Rip Van Winkle. He slouched down and bowed his head under the onslaught of my terrific nagging, rose slowly from his chair, and slunk off stage, followed by Wolf.

The second scene took place out in front, with the curtains forming a backdrop to represent the wall of the town inn. A bench was pushed through the curtains. Nicholas Vedder and Brom Dutcher, who seated themselves on the bench, were soon visited by Rip and Wolf.

The three characters sat there for some time exchanging tall tales of their hunting and fishing ventures, only to be interrupted by the shrill voice of Dame Van Winkle coming down the street in search of her erring husband. Encouraged by the applause of the first act, I assumed an air of contention and began to berate Rip and the other men with all my emotional fervor.

"Here you are, you good-for-nothing lazy hounds. Everyone of you sit around here and spit tobacco and spin yarns and leave your families at home to starve to death. You needn't laugh, Nicholas Vedder. You're the leader of this infernal band. The whole village has its eyes on you. It knows you by heart. It can tell the hour of the day by the box you're sitting on. You encourage my husband in his idleness. You brag on him for his very laziness. You're a pretty outfit, you are! A pretty outfit! A pretty outfit!"

Rip got slowly up from the bench, patted his dog on the head and mumbled to himself, "Well, Wolf, I guess we better be moving on."

While this second act had taken place, the stage behind the curtain was set for a forest scene. It is here that Rip and Wolf, on a squirrel hunting trip in the Katskill Mountains, met up with a little man and a keg of strange mountain brew. Rip becomes intrigued with Joe, who acted the part of little fellow and accepted his invitation to drink with him. More little mountain men come from behind the trees and played mumble peg to the background of distant thunder.

I was not only prompter and wardrobe mistress, I was also in charge of sound effects. I pounded on a big piece of tin back in the anteroom, which afforded a sound chamber for my thunderstorm. The thunder clashed and rumbled until the teacher signaled to me Rip had finally reeled over and fallen asleep under the potent effects of drinking from that wicked flagon.

As the curtain closed, we all helped change the stage. Virl dressed in old clothes, exchanged his gun for an old rusty piece of iron, and lay down in the spot where he had fallen asleep. We piled leaves and pine needles all over him, leaving only his torn hat and white cotton beard exposed. We exchanged the tiny evergreens for taller ones, each fastened to a cross piece of wood like a Christmas tree.

There were ohs and ahs from the audience as Rip Van Winkle slowly awoke and creakingly got to his feet. His main concern was how he was going to explain all this to Dame Van Winkle.

The final act was a village street scene with people holding a rally for George Washington, the man they wanted for their next president. Rip wandered into the crowd and identified himself as a loyal subject of the King. He was surrounded by cries of, "He's a Tory! A spy! A refugee! Get him out of here!"

Bewildered, old Rip asked for Brom Dutcher, Nicholas Vedder and Van Brummel, the schoolmaster, only to learn they were either dead or no longer living in the village. The whole affair ended happily with Rip Van Winkle being recognized by his daughter, Judith, and his son, Young Rip, who are both grown. Judith ended it all with, "Come home and live with me, Father." The curtains closed with a thunderous applause.

As the final number, everyone stood and sang the "Star Spangled Banner," including Rover, who howled on the high notes.

We had hardly gotten out of our costumes by the time the ladies were serving people with coffee, sandwiches, and cake. Some of the little children had fallen asleep and were cuddled down among the coats on the back of some desks which had been pushed against the wall.

The teacher and a group of young men were standing over by the organ. There was talk among the crowd as to whether they could have a square dance. It soon met with approval by the school board. One young fellow sprinkled corn meal about the floor to make it smooth and slick.

Martha Jones started chording on the organ, while Hiram Bailey was tuning up his fiddle. Young Pete Bailey started tapping his mouth harp against his hand and calling out, "Two more couples. Let's git rollin'. Four more couples. Let's have two squares. Come on there, Jeff. Grab yerself a woman and let's git this hoedown a-goin'."

Young Pete Bailey sang out the calls and soon the schoolhouse was alive with tapping feet and clapping hands. After several square dances, the teacher asked if the musicians could play a fox trot. A rumble of comments went throughout the crowd and the school board called a quick conference in the front hall to decide if this dance was permissible in the schoolhouse. The vote came back two to one in favor. A director on the affirmative side announced, "Well, ladies and gentlemen, Arlie and I have decided to let 'em fox trot."

Papa, with his Southern Baptist background and his reputation as a trusted member of the school board, could not go along with that decision.

"We are leaving!" And with those loud words, our family started preparing to go home. Some of the other families followed Papa's example. There was quite a commotion as children unscrambled their coats and caps.

Mama thanked Miss Coleman and complimented her on the evening's performance. "It was an excellent play and we will be looking forward to the Christmas program. Good night now."

Papa left immediately to get the horses and wagon ready to go. I reluctantly helped Mama get our belongings together. All of us with Rover, the dog, were soon riding along in the darkness.

Mama broke the silence with, "We are lucky to have a teacher who's interested in literature."

"That ain't what she's got on her mind," growled Papa, as he slapped the lines down on the horse's backs.

"Papa," called Grace from the back of the wagon. "How does a fox trot?"

"Listen, child, that's none of your affairs. There's goin' to be Hell to pay 'for I let them Hoosiers turn our schoolhouse into a roadside dance hall! I'm still clerk of that school board!"

Chapter Seventeen
The Stork Comes Back to Hawk Creek

৪০০৪

"That's a lazy man's load," came Mama's reproof as Virl went stumbling through the kitchen, hidden behind an armload of firewood. One large chunk of wood slipped to the floor as he trudged on through the dining room, leaving behind him a trail of wet snow with bits of pine bark. He dumped the wood in a corner of the living room next to the big fireplace.

Grace and I came along behind Virl with the wood stacked high across our arms. All of us old enough to carry a stick of wood participated in the chain gang chore of bringing in the fuel for cook stove, heater, and fireplace.

Joe, who was fourth in line, carried in the kindling and carefully stuffed it into a cubbyhole beneath the reservoir at the back of the kitchen range.

Each time I came in with another armload of wood, I could hear Mama reminding us, "Try to keep that door shut! Kick that snow off of your shoes! Put those dogs out!"

When the chores were finished, I brushed the snow from my coat and hung it on the metal hooks on the kitchen wall, then tossed my stocking cap up on the shelf above the coat rack. As I washed my hands, I noticed they were smudged with pitch that would not come off. There were dents along my arms from the heavy pieces of wood and a black sliver under my little fingernail. These things did not bother me for I knew Papa had turpentine to remove the pitch and the long blade of his pocket knife was a precise tool for extracting slivers.

While I set the table, Mama swept the trail of snow and bark into the dustpan and dumped it into the woodbox. All the while she was working, she was talking. "Whoever built this house didn't think of conveniences. Some people have a box where you can put the wood in from the outside. That would save a lot of this mess. Go pour the water off those potatoes and call the rest of the children to get in here or I'm going to go out there after them. It's time for supper."

After supper, Papa went into the front room to build a fire in the fireplace. The dry kindling popped as he broke it across his knee. He whittled around several pieces with his knife until they were neatly fringed with curled shavings. These he stacked in tepee-fashion against the backlog. As he kneeled before his well-constructed arrangement, Papa drew a match across the side of his tightly stretched overalls and set the kindling aflame. He was meticulous even when lighting a fire. One match did the trick and it never went out as mine always did.

Mama often gloated in the fact Papa could always build a good fire while her fire lightings were often dismal failures.

"There is an old saying you can tell the ambition of a spouse by the way a husband or wife can build a fire. With a fire like your papa makes, it shows I have ambition to spare."

"Well," commented Papa, "I don't rightly know about that ambitious idea or what in tarnation are you gitten at? All a person needs to git a far goin' is dry kindlin and some gumption. Hand me that big piece with the knot in it."

As we gathered about the fireplace, I felt that we were a happy, close-knit family. Mama looked tired as she sat there, rocking and rubbing her stomach. I had heard Papa tell someone that, come December, we were going to have one more mouth to feed. I hoped if Mama was going to have a baby, it would be a little sister.

We sat there, side by side in a little semi-circle, absorbing the warmth of the reflected flames. Part of the time we stood and revolved like puppets on a string, trying to keep both sides warm. When our backs were against the fire, we watched our grotesque shadows wiggle on the wall at the far side of the room. We spent the evening laughing and listening to our family program. Ever since the Halloween school play we looked forward to evenings when we could perform in front of the fireplace. Because of the big December snowstorm, school had been closed for two weeks and the Christmas program had been postponed.

Papa enjoyed directing our evening activities. "Well, you be first, Little Miss Muffet," he suggested, patting Grace on the head as she sat beside him in the little brown rocker.

Grace stood on the fireplace hearth with her back to the fire and curtsied, skirts held out to the side. Making appropriate gestures for each line, she recited:

"Bows on my shoulders,
Slippers on my feet,
I'm Papa's little darling.
Don't you think I'm sweet?"

The family applauded enthusiastically until it was necessary for her to give an encore.

After her second recitation, I did an Irish jig to the accompaniment of Papa's mouth harp as he played "Turkey in the Straw." I was pleased by the rhythmical sound of my feet on the cement hearth, although Papa said I must have two right feet because one of my feet did most of the jigging.

Virl used his mechanical ability to demonstrate a trick that had us all baffled.

"Who knows," commented Papa, "me and your mama might be a-raisin' another Houdini. If these youngin's keep a-practicin', who knows what might come of this. Got enough local talent fer a Chautauqua of our own."

Mama smiled and said, "Well, we don't have to practice to be actors. Remember it was Shakespeare who said, `All the world's a stage and all the men and women merely players'. It seems as if life is just one encore after another. Don't you think it is about bedtime?"

The fire was dying down. The red coals glowed in the darkening room. "Them coals look just right for popping some corn," suggested Papa, disregarding Mama's curfew. "Can't let hot coals like that go to waste."

Virl got the sack of popcorn from the back porch where it had been tied to a nail so it could freeze and become ready to explode when properly heated. I brought the long-handled black corn popper from the pantry shelf. Grace carried a big bowl and the salt shaker. We took turns shaking the popper over the hot coals. Soon we were eating and the house was fragrant with the aroma of the freshly popped corn.

"Too bad we ain't got some cider left. That salty corn makes me downright thirsty."

"Don't mention cider," interrupted Mama. "That cider you sold to that last fellow got him real tipsy before he left here."

"I reckon I ain't responsible for anyone who buys hard-cider vinegar and gets so blame thirsty he fergits all about the pickle makin'. One of you youngsters go git some apples. Let a little chewin' make your own fresh cider."

"It is still snowing," commented Virl as he came from the cellar with a pan full of crisp Ben Davis apples. For awhile, no one talked. The only sounds were the crunching of apples and the lonesome voice of the winter wind in the fireplace chimney as it drew the smoke out into the night air.

Papa put a large green log on the coals to hold the fire for the night. "Yer mama's right. It is about time for all of us to hit the hay."

On winter evenings, we were allowed to undress near the fireplace and toast our toes before going upstairs to bed.

"It is getting late," was Mama's comment as she cupped her hands around her face and peered out the window at the falling snow. "It must have been just such a night as this that Emerson wrote his poem 'The Snowstorm.' 'The housemates sit, around the radiant fire-place, enclosed in a tumultuous privacy of storm.'"

"S'pose that Emerson fellar had to split the wood and carry out the ashes?" muttered Papa, as he pushed more coals around the green log.

"Get back out of your papa's way," warned Mama. "One of you are liable to fall into that fireplace and get burned again."

Although Mama had repeatedly given warnings of the potential dangers of an open fire, both Virl and Grace had had the misfortune of stumbling into the burning coals. When Virl was a little boy, he had tripped on his trousers he was holding up to warm and had received burned fingers. Mama's first aid treatment of Watkins burn ointment left his hands without a scar.

The day Grace had burned her hands, the corner medicine cupboard contained no burn ointment, and she was left with scars on her fingers. Stories of these two incidents were frequently repeated by the neighbors and Mama's testimonials became legendary, increasing the sales of Watkins products.

"I don't feel very well," said Mama, as she started walking the floor. "Why don't you children run on up to bed."

"You heard your mama," interrupted Papa. "Let's see who can get upstairs first."

None of us wanted to be last, so we crowded out the door, around the corner and up the stairs, pushing and shoving to be first in line. As I reached the top of the stairs, I heard a thump, thump, thump of someone tumbling down the stairs.

Joe had tripped over the big brown teddy bear and had gone rolling down the stair-way and out into the dining room. The rest of us hurried back down the stairs. Mama was holding a lamp and Papa was comforting Joe.

"Who in the devil left a confounded teddy bear on the stairs? Git me a cold rag, one of ye. This here youngin's got a knot on his head as big as a hen's egg. The whole lot of ye know better to go runnin' up them stairs in the dark. Sometimes ye all act as if ye ain't got the sense God gave a goose."

After a few cold compresses, Joe was feeling better, with only a big bump on his head as evidence of his sudden descent down the stairway. Slowly we walked up the stairs, with

Joe in the lead, carrying his teddy bear. This time on our way to bed we did not care who was first or last.

I stood by the bedroom window for awhile, watching the falling snow that was silently covering the orchard with a fluffy, white blanket. The big apple trees looked ghostly as parts of the leafless branches lay bare in spots too precipitous to hold the fragile snowflakes.

As I crawled into bed, I could hear Mama's and Papa's voices in the living room below. They continued to talk for quite some time. At the sound of their voices, I felt safe and secure, an important part of a family I loved so much. I recognized the divergent backgrounds and interests of my parents, but I knew they each cherished the true worth of one another.

Meditations about my family were interrupted by the sound of someone moving furniture about downstairs. I decided to go down there and see what was going on.

Very carefully, I slipped from the bed so I would not awaken Grace. I started coughing so I could have an excuse for coming downstairs to get a drink of water. Mama and Papa were moving a bed into the living room. The fireplace fire had been rekindled and was burning brightly, lighting up the room.

"What are you doing down here?" asked Mama.

"I'm thirsty. Why are you moving the bed into this room?"

"Well, Miss Nosey," answered Papa. "If ya gotta know, yer mama is going to have a baby. It's too blamed cold in that front bedroom. Git round on tother side of this mattress and hep me fix this bed."

I was surprised by the sudden announcement and hurried to finish making the bed. Mama was sitting in the big rocker, rubbing her stomach. So that was why she had been so tired lately and why she was wearing those big Mother Hubbard dresses again.

"Papa, could I stay up and help you?"

"No, run on up to bed like a good girl. I called fer the doctor. He'll be comin' along. Ye know that telephone line got finished last fall just in time fer calls like this. I had a hard time gettin' all the folks along Hawk Creek Canyon to agree we needed telephones. Some day they'll thank me fer all the trouble I went to."

"Yes," interrupted Mama. "It's times like this we need a phone. Now you go back to bed. Papa will take care of everything. Get your sleep because I am going to need your 'elp tomorrow."

Once again in bed, I determined to stay awake and listen to all that was happening downstairs, but the quietness of the winter night soon had me dozing. When I awoke it was morning.

I ran downstairs without waiting to dress. The house was warm and smelled of Lysol. There was my Welsh grandmother standing by Mama's bed. Mama was sleeping and she looked very pale.

"Oh, Grandma, I'm so glad to see you," I exclaimed as I ran and hugged her. My worries subsided as I hid my face in my grandmother's fat neck. She smelled of talcum powder. She gave me a hug only a grandmother knows how to give.

"Come see what we 'ave in the basket. H'its a boy. Better go fetch the rest of the children so they can see the little one. Your papa is fixing some breakfast for all of you."

It did not take me long to get my brothers and my sister downstairs to see our newest baby brother. Mama was awake and smiling at us.

The baby looked pink and wrinkled. Grandma uncovered him and showed us his tiny feet. John, who was only three years old, went to Mama's bedside and asked, "Am I still the baby?"

"Yes, John, you can still be my baby, but you will have to share your things with this little brother. We are going to name him Robert. You may call him Bob if you want to," came Mama's comforting words.

Joe, who was six years old, examined the baby's little feet and hands, then walked away complaining, "That little guy couldn't lick a flea."

Grace could only say, "I wish he was a baby sister."

Grandma assured us he was a healthy baby and we should all be thankful for God's blessings. Then she remembered one of her Welsh superstitions. "This child is a late Christmas gift. This is December the twenty-ninth, and it is Friday. Remember hit's a lucky child that's born on Friday."

"That's right," added Mama. "Grandma is thinking of this verse that is called 'Monday's Child is Fair of Face'. It goes like this:

> Monday's child is fair of face,
> Tuesday's child is full of grace,
> Wednesday's child is full of woe,
> Thursday's child has far to go,
> Friday's child is loving and giving,
> Saturday's child has to work for its living,
> But the child that's born on the Sabbath day,
> Is fair and wise and good and gay."

Papa came in from the kitchen and announced that breakfast was ready and asked Grandma what she thought of his new son.

"Well, e's a Welshman if I ever saw one," said Grandma.

"Give me credit fer somethin'," came Papa's curt reply. "He may be half Welsh, but I'll tell you one thing, he's half tarheel. I'm willin' to admit, my folks was Scotch-Irish and I think that mixture should make that little baby 'bout as good as any person who ever come from the British Isles."

Chapter Eighteen
Winter of the Big Snow

ℰℭℛ

*I*t had been a long, hard winter with blizzard-like snowstorms and record-breaking cold spells. Our family felt the brunt of the season as we cleared the snow from the sagging roofs and shoveled paths so we might feed the hungry livestock. We anxiously watched the dwindling hay supply and started feeding straw from the stacks in the wheat fields.

Old timers in the neighborhoods reminded us they could remember winters with snow much deeper and mercury dipping much lower. We wondered if, perhaps, their memories were betraying them as we noticed the snowman, which we had built earlier in the winter, holding his battered head barely above the sea of white and winking at us with his one good eye while the rest of his unshapely body was hidden in the depths of the snow bank.

It had been a winter that had victimized our family and plagued us with such ailments as lumbago, neuralgia, and the grippe. With the use of such home remedies as an onion poultice for Grace's chest cold and coal oil for Virl's chilblains, we survived the rigors of the long winter and arrived at the sulphur and molasses stage with no more telltale effects than a greasy flannel pinned across the chest or an old wool sock fastened about the neck.

My complaints about the scratchy flannel brought silencing remarks from Papa. "Quit bein' sech a fussbudget. A little goose grease ain't goin' to do you no harm. Why, when I's a youngin', I had to wear assafetida around my neck month on end. That'd give you somethin' to grumble about. Had a perfume all its own, 'bout like a garlic-eatin' polecat. It was enough to scare any triflin' disease right off'n the ranch."

"You can be thankful for snow," added Mama, wiping John's nose. "There's an old sayin' that a green Christmas means a full graveyard."

"I reckon, if you're right, we don't need to worry none about these youngin's a-dying with the croup, but the way Joe's been a-coughin', you better mix up another mustard plaster. You never can tell about these Welsh superstitions; sometimes they ain't all they're cracked up to be."

Winter ailments were not confined to just us children. Mama had neuralgia from which she suffered excruciating pain. She described it as knife-like jabs of pain that stabbed at her temples. She found temporary relief with the application of a warm, moist poultice made from hops and dried peach leaves. When the pains became unbearable, she would walk the floor and moan, holding the savory poultice to her face until her cheeks were as red as roses.

Papa had more than his usual trouble with rheumatism. His hands became stiff and painful. He could no longer milk the cows, and so it was that Mama added another chore to her many daily tasks. When she discovered the chill aggravated the pains in her face, the chore of milking the cows was assigned to Virl and me. We soon made Grace our protégé of the cowshed and went about instructing her in the intricate process of extracting milk from cows.

Before the three of us left the house, Papa warned us about one old cow. "Better put the kickers on Muley. She'll kick the livin' daylights out of you if you don't watch out."

The lantern light cast shadows about us as we made our way to the barn. We were never very punctual about doing the chores. The cows, with bulging udders, mooed for relief as we entered the stable. Seated on the little one-legged stools, we began squirting the warm, white milk into the galvanized pails.

I gave Grace some last minute instructions before she began to milk Star, the most gentle of the three cows.

"Grab hold high up with the first finger and the thumb, and then with the rest of the fingers, squeeze in and pull down. It's kind of a rippling squeeze. That's right, but you have to squeeze hard if you want to get any milk. When you get that hand working, then start in with the left hand. You have to use both hands or you never will get through. Let's try it. Grab! Squeeze! Pull!"

Old Star, with her neck in the stanchion, ignored Grace's efforts and went on eating hay. I went around on the other side to milk Whitey. The noise of milk hitting the bottoms of the empty buckets resembled rain on a tin roof. The sides of the pails served to magnify the sounds. The rising contents were soon muffled as the foamy milk gradually rose toward the top.

I tied Whitey's tail to her leg so she could not flip it across my face. Virl battled it out with Muley, the breechy old cow that had to wear a neck yoke in the fields to keep her from jumping fences and hobbles at milking time to keep her from kicking out somebody's daylights.

The barnyard cats, kept as mice catchers, began to cry for their share of the steaming fresh milk. When they opened their mouths to "meow," Virl, with great accuracy, squirted streams of milk through their whiskers and down their throats. They were sorry sights as they licked the milk from their dripping fur.

Once the cats had enjoyed a taste of the warm milk, they became a nuisance at milking time. They scratched my black stockinged legs and begged for more supper. One cat mistakenly clawed the cow's leg. Whitey reacted with lightning swiftness, plunking her foot down in my pail of milk.

"There's no use crying over spilled milk," was the only consolation I could get from Virl as he finished milking Muley and came over to see how Grace was coming along.

"Haven't you got any more milk than that? You aren't even trying."

"I don't care," whimpered Grace. "I'm not planning to be a milkmaid anyway. I can't get milk out of this old cow."

"Ha! Ha!" teased Virl. "Look at the maiden, all forlorn, who milked the cow with the crumpled horn."

"Mollie, make Virl let me alone," demanded Grace, getting up from her stool and starting for the barn door.

"There goes the maiden, all forlorn, who kissed the man all tattered and torn."

"You shut up, Virl. I'm going to tell Mama on you."

"You come right back here and watch my pail so the cats don't get into it and I'll milk your blamed old cow."

When the pail was nearly full, Virl showed Grace how to strip out the last bit of milk by using the forefinger and the thumb.

"Papa says this is important. If we don't get all the milk, the cow is liable to dry up."

"I wish that one would dry up," retorted Grace. "I don't think I'll ever drink any more milk."

I noticed this was an idle threat Grace had forgotten by breakfast time when she asked, "Please pass the milk."

Virl handed her the pitcher, saying, "I thought the forlorn maiden had given up drinking this stuff."

Grace gave Virl a resounding kick under the table which brought Papa into the scene.

"None of that teasing. Remember, young man, you're at the table. And Little Miss Muffet, if I catch you kicking any more shins, I'll be obliged to lay a hand on you."

While we were at the table, Papa maintained strict discipline. "Sit up straight. This is one place you can show me your manners."

Mama taught us the rules of etiquette and Papa, making his own interpretations, enforced the rules. Being able to maintain periods of complete silence, apparently, was the main prerequisite to good manners. It took only a stern look from Papa or a warning glance from Mama to bring silence at the table.

Perhaps Grandpa started it all with his age-old philosophy that children should be seen and not heard. Mama added truth to the statement by saying silence is golden, while Papa informed us, "I think it's good fer 'em to keep their traps shut once in awhile."

While we ate in silence, we listened to Papa, who usually monopolized the table time conversations. Mama liked to discuss the things she had read about in books. Papa liked to dig into the problems of the world and solve them to his own satisfaction; therefore, Mama, along with us children, listened to the merits or demerits of women's suffrage, prohibition, and other issues of the day.

At election time, I could never decide who was campaigning the hardest, Papa or his candidate. Papa was a Republican from the South who had been schooled in the ways of defending his party against the southern Democrats and their political platform.

When I was little, I thought Democrats were children of Satan, plotting against the security of my world. I had nightmares about being pursued by those braying, two-headed monsters, only to be rescued in the nick of time by some kind-hearted gentleman leading that symbolic elephant.

It was early in the spring when Papa received a letter notifying him he was to serve on the jury in Davenport the next week. Papa considered his services on the jury not only a patriotic duty but a real privilege. He used this opportunity to help any underprivileged people who became involved in legal difficulties and whom he thought were victims of apparent injustice.

"Your papa seems to champion the underdog. He was a character witness for that young fellow who was paroled from prison. He will go anyone's bail whom he thinks stands half a chance of going straight."

Papa's remarks regarding one case led me to believe his decisions were slightly biased by the defendant's financial status.

"The last time I sat in on that jury, must have been two years ago, some bigshot was a-suin' some poor son-of-a-gun for shootin' some hounds that was a-killin' off his sheep. You could tell by lookin' at him that he didn't have nothin'. It was as plain as the nose on yer face that sheepherder didn't have a pot to wet in or a winder to sling it out of. When some poor bugger like that gits sued, I don't care what the rest of the jury thinks, I'm votin' him innocent."

Papa was to report for jury duty Monday morning. Therefore, he had to leave Sunday afternoon so he would be on time.

"This means you youngin's are goin' to have to he'p your mama around here. You'll have to trot right home from school and git at these chores," Papa instructed as he started putting some of his belongings in an old, shabby valise. "It's been a long, hard winter and this gives me a chance to earn a little extra, which'll sure come in mighty handy 'bout this time of year."

"I hate to see you leave," said Mama, handing Papa a white shirt she had just finished ironing. "We're liable to have an early thaw this spring. I noticed the air felt rather balmy today. If all this snow goes off at once, we will surely have a flood in this canyon."

"Now, I reckon it doesn't pay to borrow trouble. We'll cross that bridge when we git to it."

"What'll we do if the creek gets real high?" interrupted Virl.

"Nothin' much you can do, is there? Do like we've done in the past. Jest wait'll it goes down. I don't believe in fussin' about the weather. I jest let the good Lord take care of that. I've got enough to do a-tendin' to my own business."

Papa put on his big overcoat and his fur felt hat. He smelled of shaving soap and mothballs. He looked tired and there were new lines in his face that showed up when he was clean-shaven.

We all walked out with Papa to the barn lot when he was ready to leave. He stepped into the cutter, pulled the horsehide lap rope across his knees, and raised his arm to wave goodbye.

Old Lizzie arched her neck and stepped off at a lively trot. Her metal shoes bit into the packed snow. The runners of the sled left glistening marks on the roadway. We waved and called, "Goodbye!" until Papa was out of sight.

Mama took a handkerchief from her apron pocket and blew her nose. "There's just no use talkin' to your papa. It is just like he says: Come Hell or high water, he's going to serve on that jury and we're liable to have both of it before he gets back."

Chapter Nineteen
The Spring Flood
ಸಿಡಿ

*M*ama had various ways of forecasting the weather. Her predictions were based, least of all, on Papa's back porch barometer which consisted of a tube filled with a cloudy liquid and a gauge marked fair, changing, and stormy. The cloudy mass was invariably hanging ominously over the area marked changing. By consulting Papa's barometer, we could guess that tomorrow should be either stormy or fair, but when the next day arrived, the barometer indicated the weather, again, was changing.

Mama had other more realiable means for her predictions of the weather, such as the moon and all its cycles, verified by the printed evidence of the Farmer's Almanac with its mysterious signs of the zodiac. Each phase of the moon's cycle had its own peculiar properties for influencing life on our farm, be it person, plant, or animal.

If the new moon was a crescent, tipped to a standing position so it could contain no water, it indicated subsequent weather would be as dry as a powder horn. While if the new moon rolled on its back, capable of holding water to the brim, the rains and snows were sure to come. The seventh day of the new cycle was the ruling day and whatever the weather of that fateful twenty-four hours determined the predominating weather until the next new moon.

Along with its barometric properties for assisting in weather prediction, the moon, according to Mama, exerted a mystic power for good or evil over the Welsh and all other descendants. I was never sure if Papa was included in this exclusive group or not.

We children had learned the rules for proper behavior in the presence of the moon. Mama had handed down to us, like the storytellers of old, the family traditions and superstitions which were affected by the powers of this celestial body. If the moon had the ability to turn the tides of the oceans, which surely it did, then who were we children to doubt that the happenings in Hawk Creek Canyon were not swayed by our lunar relationship with the Old Man who inhabited that ever-changing hunk of cheese?

Perhaps it was my fault the creek flooded. I did not intend to see the new moon over my left shoulder. I was searching the skies for a star and repeating the verse: "Star light, star bright, I wish I may, I wish I might, get the wish I wish tonight." My wish was to have been that the court session would be short and Papa would return soon from jury duty. Mama had been so concerned because the weather had moderated, as she had predicted, and the spring thaw was threatening.

I did not mean to look at the moon in an indiscreet manner. Mama had told me many times that to see the first silver bow of the new moon through a window or through the branches of a tree would bring only bad luck, and if that first look was over the left shoulder, it spelled doom to be sure.

I had a blind faith in wishes, wishes that might bring a brief court session and Papa's early return home. As the daylight began to fade, I searched the sky for the evening star, when suddenly, to my surprise, just over my left shoulder, I spied the new moon squinting at me through the bare branches of the apple tree. Perhaps it was my fault the spring thaw came suddenly.

The next day a warm chinook wind was blowing through the canyon and the creek was becoming murky with the melting snow. The icicles came shattering down from the eaves and the dwindling snow fields appeared grey and dirty. The snows of the prairie, surrounding the mouth of the canyon, melted under the warm breath of the chinook. Water flowed in increasing torrents down all the valleys that joined Hawk Creek Canyon, sending the flood waters on down to the Columbia River.

By the time the waters reached our place, the creek had grown to sudden proportions. At nightfall it was a roaring torrent, rumbling in the dark and slowly creeping higher up the banks, a monstrous glutton pulling away the cultivated soil of Papa's farm.

We went to bed late that night, wooed to sleep by the unceasing grumbling of the flooding waters. I slept fitfully, waking often to listen to the steady roar of the stream I knew was up to the edge of the yard and lapping against the back of the woodshed. I shuddered as I recalled how easily the rising creek had taken the footbridge we used to cross over to go to Uncle's place. It had been swept away like a toy boat, twisting end for end in a helpless manner. I could hear Mama walking about downstairs and I wished Papa were home from jury duty.

I fell asleep again, only to dream. It was a nightmare of incoherent happenings in which I was very much like the boy at the dike in Holland, attempting to hold back the flood. No matter how I tried, the muddy waters pushed me through the swimming hole and on across our favorite sandbar, sweeping with it our secret tunnels and beautiful sand castles. As I ran on, with the water right at my heels, I picked up a mother killdeer and her nest full of little ones and held them close against me. I awoke with a jolt to find myself tangled in the quilts of my bed and my heart pounding in my ears.

It was then I heard the back door close and Mama coming to the foot of the stairs. "Children! Wake up! I'm going to need your help. Do you hear me? The bank is caving in back of the barn and it looks as if the granary is going to go."

I got out of bed in a hurry. I went across the hall and called Virl and Joe. Grace and I dressed quickly and went downstairs, carrying our shoes and stockings. Mama looked tired and worried. She had on her big overshoes and was holding a lighted lantern.

"We'll have to get the seed grain out of that building. If any more of that bank gives way, the whole granary is liable to go. I hate to take you children out there, but we are going to have to do something. We can't just stand here. I don't see what your Papa ever meant going away and leaving us at a time like this."

Grace and Joe, who were up and dressed, were left at the house to be with John and the baby, who were still sleeping.

"There's plenty of wood in the heater," advised Mama, "so don't bother the fire. I nursed the baby about half an hour ago so he should sleep for awhile, but if you need me, just come to the door and holler. If you're hungry, you can fix yourself some bread and milk."

It was only on rare occasions Mama ever left any of us alone in the house. She reluctantly shut the door on the four younger children and hurried toward the barnyard, with Virl and me tagging along behind.

The coal oil lantern cast a faint gleam out toward the roaring flood waters. We were alone and helpless against this mighty force. There was a margin of land still left behind the buildings, but it was obvious that large portions of the barnlot had given way to the onslaught of the swirling maelstrom and then striking out across the valley in search of another target.

As we stood there in silence, another chunk of bank cracked and slid down into the water. The flood was undermining a path directly toward the granary and our supply of seed wheat, which Papa had stored in readiness for the spring planting.

As Mama surveyed the situation, she began to pray. "Dear God, I need your help. Give me strength. God protect us. This is dangerous."

Then Mama turned and warned us, "I need your help. Listen to me! We must be careful. Let's go get the team and wagon."

The certainty of what obviously was going to happen goaded us into action. We harnessed the team, hitched them to the wagon, and backed it up to the granary door. Fortunately, the floor of the building was several steps up from the ground so it was possible for us to lay some boards across from floor to wagon bed.

It was a most difficult task for us to move the heavy burlap sacks of grain. Papa had them stacked in neatly spaced tiers against the back wall. The urgency of the situation apparently gave us added strength as we pulled the big sacks down from the piles and rolled them across the floor and into the wagon.

It was with great effort the horses moved the heavily loaded wagon across the barnlot to a safe distance from the flood. Although we were nearly exhausted, we put the horses in the barn and hurried back to remove Papa's farm implements out of the shed, which was a lean-to on the side of the granary.

We carried the tools across the barnyard and left them by the orchard fence. I dragged the heavy crowbar behind me, running as I went and praying for time to rescue Papa's valuable supply of farm equipment. These were the implements Papa had used for clearing away the brush and trees so he might look across the broad expanse of clean, uncluttered meadows and farmland.

As I hurried through the night, my way but dimly lighted by the far-off flickering lantern, I realized the tools I was carrying had been used to clear a path for the flood. Mama had told Papa she thought that willows, thorns, and other trees, with their deeply imbedded roots, should be left to grow because they were nature's way of holding the soil. Mama's advice had gone unheeded. Papa had cleared the creek banks and turned the natural meadows to richly cultivated wheat fields that lay soft and defenseless.

The sounds of the flooding water rumbled about me as I hung the large and small mattocks through the boards of the orchard fence. These were the grubbing tools that had left the land vulnerable to the onslaught of the eroding flood waters that laughed in the night as they mocked Papa's neatness and laid waste to the fruits of his back-breaking labor.

As I went back again for some more tools, I passed Virl carrying a pevee and a posthole digger. Mama came struggling along with a cant hook and a buck saw. When I reached the doorway, I was startled to see a hole in the corner with the water lapping greedily at the earthen floor. I screamed. Virl and Mama soon stood beside me. We were all trembling as we looked at the gaping hole where only moments before we had been standing.

"Let's go to the house," said Mama wearily, as she took the lantern down from a hook on the doorway of the building. "We're lucky to be alive."

Dawn was breaking in the east as we passed the pile of tools and went through the orchard gate. The kitchen door opened and Joe ran out on the porch, calling, "Mama, Mama, come quick."

All of us ran, expecting something dreadful to be happening. When we entered the kitchen, Grace was sweeping and Joe was holding the dustpan. "Grace broke the sugar bowl," announced Joe.

Turning to me, Mama said, "You go fix the children some breakfast and I'll go tend to the baby."

It was nearly noon when Papa came home that morning. Since the roads were almost bare and the sled had to be left in town, he had ridden home with a neighbor with Old Lizzie tied behind the wagon.

We went out to meet Papa and soon our family was assembled in the barn lot. We discussed the possible ways of saving the granary, which was sitting precariously on the bank of the flooding creek. There was mention of anchoring the building with ropes or cables. Then came the realization our suggestions were only impossibilities, for it would necessitate an engineering task, which for us would be completely impossible.

The flood had crested, but the bank along the barn lot continued to cave in. Papa looked bewildered and helpless as he surveyed the devastating effects of the flooding water. The main current had undermined the banks of the fields at every turn of the creek. As the swift water knifed its way along, huge wedges of the fertile soil trembled and then slowly crumbled forward into the muddy stream.

As we stood talking, arguing, and trying to solve the problem of saving the granary, the building suddenly shuddered, tipped sideways, then hesitated a moment before slipping into the moving water. It kept afloat as it bobbled crazily about, turning round and round, out into the main current and down the creek. It went on past the orchard and down by the woodshed. We ran along, watching until it went out of sight.

Grace and I were crying. I was afraid. I remembered how the moon had winked at me through the apple tree before the chinook wind had started to blow. Mama then spoke, as if to herself. "I've noticed that the land that isn't cleared never washes like this. If you'd only left the trees and the brush along the creek bank. If we'd only...."

"If! If! If!" exclaimed Papa. "If the dog hadn't stopped for the fence post, he'd a-caught the rabbit. I can't he'p it if my foresight ain't as good as my hindsight."

Papa walked to the house ahead of us. His good, dark suit was wrinkled and his shoulders stooped more than usual. Mama stood in the yard awhile, stunned by the awfulness of the flood.

Mama picked up John, who was tugging at her skirts. She kissed the top of his head and he nuzzled against her as he enjoyed the security of her protecting arms.

"You know, children," reflected Mama, "I don't think your papa was ever cut out to be a farmer. Seems he doesn't realize it, though...remember, it was Bobby Burns who said, ` Oh wad some Power the giftie gie us, To see oursels as ithers see us!'" Then Mama laughed rather strangely and added, with tears in her voice, "Well, maybe I wasn't cut out to be a farmer's wife, either."

"Grandma says we would have good luck if we put a horseshoe over the door," I suggested, remembering soberly it was I who had seen the new moon through the trees, a new moon that had laughed at me with the warm breath of a chinook wind. Now was the time to try a horseshoe for good luck.

"Perhaps you children will be finding horseshoes when the flood water goes down. If you like, I'll put them over every single door in the house."

"We might find some," added Virl, "but I'll bet you a dollar to a doughnut they'll be fastened to a dead horse."

We ignored Virl's comment as we heard the door open and saw Papa come out of the house. He held his arms behind him and called to us children, "I brought you somethin' mighty good from town. Which hand do you want? The right or the left'n?"

Papa had not forgotten the horehound candy or the pink peppermints. John was the first to get to choose. Mama and Papa laughed when John said, "I'll take both hands," and then grabbed Papa around the neck and gave him a big hug and a kiss, saying, as he drew back quickly from Papa's whiskered face, "You got pins in your chin, Papa."

Papa handed the candy to Mama and threw John up on his shoulders so he was sitting astride his neck.

Now that Papa was home, I knew everything would be all right. Papa always knew what to do. We no longer needed a horseshoe over the door.

Chapter Twenty
Leaving Hawk Creek Canyon

৯০৫৪

*H*aving survived the flood and realizing Mama's predictions on the weather by looking at the moon and its cycles kept Virl and me looking at the moon every night. To this day, I don't understand the zodiac, but I truly believe God has a hand in it.

Mama always said that by believing in God, Christ, and the Bible's teaching, you can't go wrong. Even Uncle Gus would say, "God changed the barometric pressure and my arthritis is killing me. What did I ever do wrong?"

As spring came and with Papa being home, I was sure the worst in life was behind our family until one day, Mama came inside the house. With a very serious look on her face, she said, "Mollie, you need to go out and see Papa right away." I was sure something was wrong, and as I ran to see Papa, who was in the barn, I thought maybe one of the boys was in trouble. As I reached the barn door, I said nervously in a low voice, "Papa, Mama said you wanted to talk to me."

In his best Southern drawl, Papa spoke words I could tell were hard to come out. He said to me, "Mollie, I just got word that my pa has died. I think we should go down to Yakima and see your grandma." The look on his face when he said, "How would you like to stay with your grandma and go to high school in Yakima?" told me the die was cast and I was going to care for my grandma and go to high school in Yakima. "You better go get your things packed, girl. Your Uncle Press will be here in the morning to take us to Yakima."

What a scary thought for a country girl to leave home and go to a strange town and a strange school. I had heard the school didn't have one room like I was used to. Each subject was taught in a different room and the school was three stories high. I stayed up most of the night, imagining all kinds of dreadful things.

We had no suitcase, just an old, large, wooden box to pack my clothes into. In the morning, Virl carried it out to the road for me. After saying goodbye to old Lizzie, I approached Papa, who was standing by the road, waiting for Uncle Press to show up in his new Model A pick-up. I asked, "Papa, why can't my cousins, who live right down the road from Grandma, take care of her? You need me here."

"Never you mind, daughter." (He never called me daughter.) "Your cousins got no lick of sense and can't hardly take care of themselves."

When Uncle Press drove up, Papa picked up my box and yelled, "Mollie, hurry up and hug and kiss your little brothers and sister goodbye." As I hugged Mama, she had tears in her eyes as she told me, "Now you be a good girl when you're down there."

With no fanfare, Papa said, "You and the box go in the back of the pick-up. Your mama has packed us a lunch. Now hurry up. We have a long trip ahead of us."

The pick-up started out to the main road. I looked back, waving to my family, and Mama yelled one more time, "You be a good girl and help your grandma down there!"

As the Model A rounded the last bend in the road, I looked back and realized for the first time that Hawk Creek, the house, and even the barn looked very special to me.